ONE HUNDRED MERRY MEMORIES

AN ASPEN COVE SMALL TOWN ROMANCE

KELLY COLLINS

BOOK NOOK PRESS

Copyright © 2023 by Kelley Maestas

No part of this publication may be reproduced, distributed, or transmitted in any form or by any means, including photocopying, recording, or other electronic or mechanical methods, without the prior written permission of the publisher, except as permitted by U.S. copyright law. For permission requests, contact kelly@authorkellycollins.com.
The story, all names, characters, and incidents portrayed in this production are fictitious. No identification with actual persons (living or deceased), places, buildings, and products is intended or should be inferred. All products or brand names are trademarks of their respective owners.

FOREWORD

Dear Reader,

Welcome back to our cherished town! "One Hundred Merry Memories" is your invitation to reminisce with familiar folks and relive moments that made us all laugh, cry, and cheer.

Writing this book has been like flipping through an old photo album, each page a snapshot of the people and events that make Aspen Cove so special. I've poured my heart into capturing these memories, and I hope you'll find the same joy in reading them as I did in writing them.

So settle in and take a stroll down memory lane with me. Thank you for being such an important part of my journey.

Happy Reading!
Kelly Collins

CHAPTER ONE

Amanda Anderson sat at her small, cluttered desk, hunched over her laptop, attempting to find inspiration to write her novel. The city apartment was cramped, with the sounds of blaring horns, construction, and the general chaos of urban life filtering through the thin walls. She sighed, running her fingers through her messy hair, trying to block out the din and focus on her writing. No matter how much she tried, the words wouldn't come.

She glanced around her place, taking in the remnants of the life she once shared with Daniel. The stark white walls were adorned with mismatched frames, filled with memories of happier times. The potted plants she had tended to with such care now drooped, their leaves turning a sickly shade of yellow. What was a sanctuary was now suffocating.

A wave of sadness overwhelmed her as she thought about the breakup. It had been a few months since he left, but the pain was fresh, like an open wound. The relationship had disintegrated, leaving Amanda emotionally raw and creatively drained. She couldn't find the motivation to do what she loved most—write.

Her eyes wandered to the window, where the city skyline loomed large, a constant reminder of the chaos outside her door. She longed for the peace that was so elusive in her current environment. "Maybe a change of scenery would help," she murmured, unsure if she believed it.

The cursor on her laptop screen blinked impatiently, waiting for her to type anything, but the blank page mocked her. She closed her eyes, trying to summon the characters and settings that had once come so easily. She imagined a quaint small town, nestled among snow-capped mountains, with charming cottages and friendly neighbors. The contrast between her imaginary world and the harsh reality was striking.

Opening her eyes, she pushed herself away from the desk, standing up to stretch her stiff limbs. She moved across the room, while her orange tabby, Catsby, ran figure eights around her legs.

"Hey boy, are you restless too?"

Catsby wasn't a meowing type of cat but a trilling one who let out a long warble as if to answer her question. The problem was that she didn't speak feline, so she didn't know if he agreed or disagreed.

She walked over to the window and gazed at the landscape below. Cars were lined bumper-to-bumper, horns honking, people yelling. She leaned her forehead against the cool glass and tried to block the noise out.

Her thoughts drifted back to her breakup; doubts and questions swirled through her mind, a cyclone of emotion that threatened to overwhelm her. She tried to calm herself by taking a deep breath, but the tightness in her chest persisted, constantly reminding her of the heartache that had become her new normal.

Overwhelmed with the desire to escape the confines of her apartment, she grabbed her coat and slipped on her shoes. The brisk autumn air nipped at her cheeks as she stepped outside and wrapped her jacket tighter around her body. She roamed the streets of Chicago. As she continued to wander, she was drawn to a small park tucked away between towering buildings. It was a tiny oasis of green in the center of the concrete jungle, and Amanda experienced a flicker of hope as she entered its gates. The sounds of the city faded away, replaced by the rustling of branches and the gentle chirping of birds.

She sat on a secluded bench beneath an enormous oak tree, breathing in the earthy scent of damp soil and fallen leaves. A calm covered her for the first time in an eternity. Surrounded by nature, she granted herself permission to exist without the weight of her worries and heartache.

Sitting there, the seeds of a story began to take root. She envisioned a woman, similar to herself, seeking solace and inspiration in a small town far away from city life's chaos. The town's residents welcomed her with open arms, and she found the peace she'd been craving, a sense of belonging, and the possibility of love.

Amanda smiled as it unfolded in her mind, her heart swelling with fresh hope and creativity. She knew she couldn't stay in this park forever and would have to return to her apartment, but for now, she allowed herself to get lost in her fantasy. And it was just that because after Daniel, she no longer believed in love, fairytales, or happily ever after, but she could write them for others to enjoy.

With renewed determination, she stood and returned to her place, her soul lighter and her mind filled with possibilities.

At her desk, the sounds of the city outside her window

seemed louder than before, a cacophony of noise that threatened to drown out her thoughts.

With her fingers poised over her laptop's keyboard, she tried to recapture the peace she'd experienced beneath the oak tree, but as she stared at the blank document on her screen, her frustration grew. The words that had been so clear and vivid in the park now escaped her.

Discouraged, she closed her laptop and picked up her phone. In times like these, she needed her best friend, Meg. She dialed her number and waited.

"What's up, buttercup?" Meg joked in her usual carefree tone.

"Ugh," Amanda groaned. "This life of mine. I'm struggling right now."

Meg's voice softened with empathy. "Let me have it. I'm all ears."

"It's like one minute I'm walking, and suddenly, boom! I hit a wall, you know? Nothing brings me happiness anymore, and I can't seem to get my creative juices flowing. What am I supposed to do?"

Meg listened as Amanda vented. "Girl, I feel ya. Breakups are no joke. But I promise you things will get better. You're strong, and you'll get through this."

Despite Meg's encouragement, Amanda was lost. "I want something that will point me in the right direction, you know?"

Meg let out a warm laugh. "Hey, it's time for you to get up and go. You can't sit here in the remnants of your last relationship. I bet you still have his picture on the wall."

Amanda frowned. "It's true. He's still there."

"What you need is a major change. Let's start with you purging Daniel from your life."

"But he was such a big part of it."

"And he's gone. What about a vacation?"

"I can't go anywhere. I'm working on a novel."

"Are you? How much have you completed?"

She looked down at her blank screen and typed, "Once upon a time...."

"I have a few words."

"Liar." She could almost see Meg roll her eyes. "'Once upon a time' doesn't count."

"Yes, it does. Every fairytale starts with it."

"You don't write fairytales; you pen romance."

"Same thing."

"He did a number on you."

"Geez, Meg, what guy takes you to the swankiest restaurant in town to tell you he's leaving you?"

"It happened in *Legally Blonde*."

She couldn't argue. Her life had mimicked art right down to Daniel's words, "Oh, you thought I was going to propose? How sweet."

"I'm never falling in love again."

"Not every man is a Daniel. You can't punish the whole of the male species because the one you had was a douchebag. Get back on that horse, sweetie."

"I don't know. But you're correct about one thing. I can't keep doing the same things and expect a different outcome."

"So do something completely out of character. Get a new apartment or come to Miami and live with me."

She thought about the hustle and bustle of Miami. "Similar problems, different city. Bigger bugs and gators. No thanks. Look, I'm turning off my lights and closing the blinds. Catsby is racing by me to lay claim to my pillow. Thanks for always having my back. I love you."

She hung up and looked at the wall of memories. Meg was right. It was time to purge the past. She dragged over the trashcan and tossed every picture with Dan in it. He was no longer a part of her life and had no business in her home.

If she were being honest, it wasn't him that she missed. It was this feeling of belonging to someone or something.

A soft warble came from her room. Catsby was calling.

"I'm coming."

She got ready for bed and pushed her cat from her pillow before crawling under the covers. When she closed her eyes, she said a silent prayer. "Please, give me a sign. Show me what I'm supposed to do next."

With that, she drifted to sleep, hoping tomorrow would bring her the answers she desperately needed.

SHE AWOKE THE FOLLOWING DAY, her conversation with Meg and the whispered devotion still fresh in her mind. Her mail slot opened, and a pile of papers hit the ground. Her eyes landed on a tattered pink envelope. The return address was from a B. Bennett, and the name immediately struck a chord in her memory. Brandy Bennett had been her pen pal when she was in seventh grade. They had written to each other for years, sharing stories of their lives and dreams for the future. But, like so many childhood friendships, they had lost touch.

Curiosity piqued, Amanda examined the envelope more closely, noticing the numerous forwarding stickers layered on top of one another. She wondered why it had taken so long to reach her.

Settling on the sofa, she peeled the labels away, revealing that it had been forwarded several times. She had moved around a lot after meeting Daniel until they had settled in Chicago a year ago.

She opened the tattered envelope, pulling out several neatly folded pages. The handwriting was elegant, and as she began reading, she discovered it was from Bea Bennett, Brandy's mother.

Dear Amanda,

I hope this letter finds you well, though I know it has been years since you last corresponded with my daughter, Brandy. My name is Bea Bennett, and I am Brandy's mother. I wanted to take the time to reach out to you and express my sincere thanks for the kindness you shared with Brandy during your time as pen pals.

I regret to inform you that Brandy passed away several years ago. She often spoke of the letters she exchanged with you. Your friendship meant a great deal to her. Even though you lost touch, I know she carried the memory of you in her heart.

I'm now in the twilight of my life and have been reflecting on the people who have touched our lives. It's essential to acknowledge your role in Brandy's and to offer you a token of my appreciation. Enclosed with this letter is the deed to a charming cabin in Aspen Cove. It is an amazing, small town that has provided comfort and a sense of belonging to those who have come to call it home.

If you take a chance on Aspen Cove, you will find everything a person could ask for. Bring the paperwork to Doc Parker, who will help you settle into our little piece of paradise.

Again, thank you for the kindness and joy you brought to my daughter's life. I hope Aspen Cove can offer you the same serenity and happiness it has given many others.

Warm regards,

Bea Bennett

AMANDA HELD the letter in her hands with mixed emotions. She was heartbroken that Brandy had passed. Her life was cut so short. Despite the sad news, the page was filled with kindness and love. She couldn't believe the incredible turn her life had taken. Excitement and intrigue welled up within her, making her wonder if this was the sign she had asked for.

She said a silent prayer of thanks for the opportunity to have known Brandy and the gift her mother Bea had bestowed upon her at the exact time she needed a miracle.

She carried the pages over to her desk, opening her laptop to research the town. Images of quaint, picturesque streets, charming storefronts, and cozy homes filled the screen, and it tugged at her heart. It was as if the place was calling out to her, inviting her to leave behind the chaos of the city and find solace in its peaceful embrace.

Unable to contain her joy, she rushed to call Meg.

"Oh my gosh! You won't believe what happened!"

"Whoa, calm down. Tell me what's up," Meg said.

Amanda filled her in on the details of the pink letter, Brandy, and Bea Bennett's generous gift. She spoke faster as she told the story, afraid she wouldn't get it all out before she woke from a dream, or someone came to tell her it was all a mistake.

"That's incredible! It's like fate or something—you asked for a sign, and the universe answered in spades."

Amanda laughed. "I know ... it's so wild. I'm still trying to wrap my head around everything, but I think I'll do it. I'm moving to Aspen Cove."

"Yes! Yes, yes, yes!" Meg cheered from the other end of

CHAPTER TWO

Jackson awoke early, his body still syncing with the military clock ingrained in him over the years. The golden glow of the morning sun streamed through the curtains, casting a warm light across the room. He stretched, his muscles protesting from the previous day's work at Bishop's Brewhouse moving cases of beer and spirits. A soft whine drew his attention to the foot of the bed where his loyal German Shepherd, Gunner, sat patiently, his tail wagging nonstop.

"Alright, buddy, let's go for our walk," Jackson murmured, swinging his legs over the side of the bed, and standing. The worn wooden floorboards beneath his bare feet contrasted with the rough concrete and metal of the barracks he'd left behind.

He brushed his teeth, dressed, and laced up his boots, while the memories of his time in the Army played like a slideshow. The grueling training, the strong bonds he'd formed with his fellow soldiers, and the harsh reality of the missions he'd been sent on. Among those he'd grown closest to was Bowie, a man who'd become like a brother to him.

the line. "This is going to be amazing for you—reinvigorating. A fresh start, a new adventure. I'm so excited for you!"

She hung up with renewed determination and started planning her relocation to Colorado. She contacted her landlord, gave notice, organized her belongings, and made a list of all the things she'd need to do before leaving the city behind.

She could already picture herself sitting by a roaring fire in her living room, the snow falling gently outside as she worked on her latest novel. At that moment, she knew Aspen Cove was where she was meant to be.

They'd been through the worst of it together and had come out the other side mostly whole.

They exited through the patio door of his room at B's Bed and Breakfast. Gunner bounded excitedly ahead as they stepped outside, the brisk morning air nipping at Jackson's cheeks. The dog looked at the lake, which was already starting to ice over.

"Not today, boy. It's too cold." Jackson zipped his camouflage jacket up to his neck and headed toward the heartbeat of Aspen Cove. The picturesque streets were bathed in the early light, making Main Street sweeter. The town was still asleep, everything quiet and peaceful, and a welcome change from his past life.

As he walked, he couldn't help but contrast the serenity around him with the cacophony of his past life—where the air had been thick with the acrid smell of gunpowder, and the nights shattered by the relentless percussion of artillery fire. Here, the only battle was against the morning cold, and for that, he was grateful.

The temperature was a far cry from the stifling confines of the barracks or the dusty, oppressive air of the war zones he'd been deployed to.

He breathed deeply, savoring the scent of pine trees and the faint smell of sizzling bacon and pancakes from Maisey's Diner.

Gunner's ears perked up at the sound of birdsong, his head tilting curiously at the melody that surrounded them.

Jackson smiled at the simple joy his canine companion found in these small moments.

His thoughts drifted to Bowie and the life he had built here. He married Katie, a woman with a heart as big as the mountains surrounding them and one belonging to Bowie's former fiancée, Brandy. What were the chances of falling in love with the same heart twice? There was magic here, and Bowie getting injured in the war now seemed more of a blessing than a curse. It brought him back to the family business and allowed him to meet his wife.

The Bishop brothers were why he was here. They provided a place for him to land and transition into civilian life. Bowie ran the family's tackle shop, while his brother, Cannon, managed the local bar. The two businesses were situated side by side, becoming a popular gathering spot for the townspeople.

Jackson's work at Bishop's Brewhouse was fulfilling in its way, but he couldn't shake the sense that there was something more he needed. He missed the camaraderie and sense of purpose he'd had in the Army, the shared goals that bound them all together. It was a feeling he hadn't quite been able to replicate in his current life.

Jackson wondered what the future held for him. He knew he was lucky to have found a place like Aspen Cove where he could begin to heal and find his footing once more.

The townsfolk had a way of providing what people needed before they knew they needed it, and he had faith that, in time, he, too, would discover his forever here.

The town slowly stirred as they continued—the signs of life emerging with lighted storefronts. He could smell the first batch of muffins baking at B's Bakery, mingling with the scent of woodsmoke from the chimneys of nearby homes.

Jackson walked past the bait and tackle store and spotted Bowie standing in front, unloading a heavy wooden box from his truck. He stopped and waved. "Hey, man," he called, approaching his friend. "Need some help with that?"

Bowie looked at the crate and then back at Jackson, his grin widening. "I'd appreciate it."

The two carried it into the shop and set it down by the counter. "What's in there, anyway?" Jackson asked,

Bowie chuckled, wiping the sweat from his brow. "Just some supplies for the upcoming ice fishing season. It'll be here before we know it. We have to get a hard freeze before they can ice fish, but I want to be ready."

Jackson nodded, understanding the importance of preparing for the seasonal changes in Aspen Cove. "Yeah, I can imagine it gets pretty lively here when that time rolls around."

"You bet." Bowie clapped Jackson on the back. "But it's also a great time for the town to unite. Winter is best enjoyed with cups of hot cocoa and long talks by the fire. It's also when Maisey makes biscuits and gravy and her famous pumpkin pies."

Jackson smiled, appreciating how the small town came together during the various seasons. It was a far cry from barracks life. "Well, if you need help getting ready, let me know. I'm always here to lend a hand."

Bowie's eyes crinkled as his lips lifted into a smile. "Thanks, Jackson. I appreciate that. But for now, enjoy your day. I've got this covered."

With a nod, Jackson left the tackle shop and walked across the street into Maisey's Diner, the bell above the door announcing his arrival with a cheerful jingle. He took a deep breath, inhaling the familiar scents of home-cooked goodness.

"Mornin', Jackson." Maisey's face was creased with a lifetime of laughter lines, her weathered hands pouring him a cup of steaming coffee and setting it in front of his normal seat.

"The usual?" she asked.

"You know me too well," he replied with a grin, sitting at the counter.

While waiting for his breakfast, Jackson overheard the chatter of the locals around him. The conversation turned to the storm and the upcoming Thanksgiving Day feast the town had planned at the Guild Creative Center.

When Maisey brought his eggs, pancakes, and bacon, she sat beside him. "What's shakin'?" she asked.

"Same stuff, different day." Maisey always gave him an extra slice of bacon that he slipped to Gunner, who lay by his feet anticipating his treat. "Just working at the bar and hanging with Gunner." He chowed down on his meal, still not accustomed to having all the time in the world to eat.

"All work and no play makes Jackson a dull boy."

"There's something to be said for a low-key life." He'd had enough adrenaline rushes for a lifetime. Nothing got the blood pumping like an exploding IED or an air raid siren.

"That there is," Maisey agreed, patting his hand fondly before collecting his empty plate and heading back into the kitchen.

Jackson finished his coffee and thanked Maisey then placed money on the counter and took Gunner out for their usual morning walk. Everywhere they went, people waved in greeting, acquaintances quickly becoming friends as time passed in Aspen Cove.

He talked with Katie, who was setting up her holiday decorations. Gunner sniffed around happily, then looked at Katie with his give-me-a-treat look.

"You already had bacon, buddy. You don't get something at every stop."

Katie laughed. "Oh yes, he does. Do you think my pup Bishop comes for a visit and doesn't get a goody?"

Bishop was her and Bowie's chocolate lab and one of Gunner's fur friends. Katie rushed into the bakery and returned with a bone-shaped treat.

"I tried a new recipe. This is peanut butter, and Bishop goes gaga for them." She held out her hand in the command Gunner knew as sit, and the dog planted his back end on the cold sidewalk, patiently waiting for Katie to offer the goods. When she did, he took it from her hand and scarfed it up in seconds flat. He, too, was a product of army life and uncertain futures.

Jackson looked at the greenery Katie was hanging. "Is Christmas a big deal here?"

She smiled and then sighed. "I'm working on them. The first year I was here, they didn't hang a single light, scrap of garland, or a wreath." She peeked around him and pointed to the roundabout at the end of Main Street. "Don't you think it would be amazing if we put a giant tree in the center with thousands of lights? We could have a lighting ceremony. Drink cocoa and sing carols."

Christmas had always been special for Jackson, even more so when he was in the army. When he was far from home, care packages would show up. These boxes, sent to "any soldier," were filled with letters, cards, and homemade goodies.

Opening these packages felt like getting a hug from home. A pair of knitted socks wasn't just fabric; it was warmth in a cold barracks. A homemade cookie wasn't just sugar and flour; it was a taste of home, a momentary escape from the relentless demands of duty.

Each item from those boxes lifted his spirits, especially when he missed his family and friends the most. They were simple things, but they meant the world to him when he was far away.

"I think that would be great," he said wistfully, looking away. "Doesn't everyone want that?"

She shrugged. "They do. They just don't know it yet."

"Let me know what I can do," he offered.

She smiled, her eyes lifting, causing her brows to disappear under her bangs. "Oh, sugar, don't offer if you're not ready to follow through." She laughed. "You know the saying 'ask, and ye shall receive?' That's my motto in life—I'm all about the asking. If I ask, I expect the receiving part to follow."

Jackson left the bakery and crossed the street, his eyes meeting Marina's from Cove Cuts as he approached. She and her daughter Kellen were in the process of decorating a window with holiday cheer.

"Mornin' Jackson," Marina said. He smiled and kneeled next to the small girl. Pinned to her chest was a junior sheriff badge, and holstered at her hips were two plastic squirt guns.

Kellen wrapped her thin arms around Gunner's neck and squeezed, burying her face in the animal's fur. Gunner nuzzled her cheek. She giggled and sank to her knees. Jackson grinned. Life didn't get any better than this.

LATER THAT DAY, Jackson strode into the warm, inviting atmosphere of the brewhouse, his boots clicking on the wooden floor as he approached the bar. The low hum of friendly chatter and laughter filled the air as patrons enjoyed their drinks and each other's company. The smell of hops and pine cleaner drifted through the space. It was a weird combination but oddly comforting.

Behind the counter, Bowie was pouring a pint of ale for Doc, his movements practiced and fluid. He glanced up and spotted Jackson, greeting him with a nod. "Hey, man. Good timing. Cannon's out tonight, so I'm helping out."

Cannon, who ran the business, had been struggling lately. He was burning the candle at all ends with the schedule he kept. He stocked the bar during the day while trying to do maintenance work on the inn and care for his wife and son. Jackson imagined *his* presence at the inn didn't make things easier. He always tried to be helpful but having someone underfoot in the house had to be tough. Especially for newer parents.

"Bowie, I appreciate everything Sage and Cannon have done for me, letting me stay at the bed and breakfast," Jackson began hesitantly. "But I can't shake the feeling that I'm intruding on their family life, you know?"

Bowie nodded, seeming to understand where his friend was coming from. "They've been happy to have you there, but it's natural to want your own space."

"Would they receive new guests if I wasn't there?" The wing of the house he was staying in had remained vacant since his arrival despite having several rooms to rent.

Bowie shook his head. "They decided not to take on anyone until the little guy is older."

He figured as much. He wasn't a paying guest and saw all the trouble they went through to make him feel welcome and comfortable.

"Maybe it's time for me to get out of their way."

Bowie glanced at him. "Jackson, I get it, I really do. You see the lengths my family takes to make you feel at home and you question your place. But know this, they don't see you as a burden."

As Bowie spoke, his gaze wandered over to Doc, who occupied the last bar stool, nursing his beer. "If you genuinely wish to strike out on your own, I'll stand by you. In fact, Doc over there can help you find a new space to call home. Besides winning at tic-tac-toe, and lending an ear, he's got a knack for real estate. Oh, and if you're in the mood for tying the knot, he can officiate that too."

Jackson wiped down the bar top, chuckling. "I'll start laying down roots with a home. I'm not in the market for a wife."

Doc's eyebrows rose as he said, "You don't have to be, son. When the time is right, women have an instinct that lets them know you're ready."

Jackson raised an eyebrow, amused by Doc's comment. "Is that so?"

"Absolutely," Doc replied, his voice warm and wise. "When you least expect it, love has a way of sneaking up on you. Trust me, I've seen it happen more times than I can count."

The door opened, and a dark-haired woman entered. She looked around the room, eyes scanning the patrons before they settled on Doc. Jackson noticed her striking features and bright smile, and he found it difficult to tear his gaze away.

"Excuse me," she said sweetly, approaching them. "I'm looking for Doc Parker."

Doc beamed at her, extending a hand. "That would be me, ma'am. And you are?"

"I'm Amanda Anderson," she replied, shaking his hand. "I received this letter." She pulled the pink envelope from her bag. "I was told to bring it to you."

Doc's eyes widened with surprise as he took the envelope from her. "Well, I'll be. I was wondering when another one would show up."

"Another one?" Amanda asked.

Doc nodded. "Yes, Bea Bennett had a habit of sending those to folks she thought could benefit from coming to Aspen Cove. So, what brings you to our little town?"

Amanda hesitated before explaining her situation and the unexpected gift from Bea. Doc listened, nodding in understanding.

"Well, you've been given a wonderful opportunity." Doc smiled. "I can give you directions. It's up in the mountains, a lovely spot." He drew her a rudimentary map, on a napkin, that would get her there.

As Amanda started to leave, Doc, with a grandfatherly concern, raised an important question. "Now, Miss Anderson, have you arranged the utilities at the property? Power, water, and such?"

There was a proud glint in her eyes. "Yes, I took care of all that before I left Chicago. I didn't want to arrive and find myself in the dark, especially in an unfamiliar place."

Doc nodded approvingly. "That's very wise of you. It's always good to be prepared."

Amanda blushed at his comments. "Well, I try my best to plan."

Doc patted her on the arm. "That's the spirit, young lady. It'll serve you well here in Aspen Cove. Don't hesitate to reach out if you need help or have any questions. We're a close-knit group and take care of our own."

"Thank you so much." Amanda's eyes filled with emotion. She turned to leave, but not before giving Jackson a polite nod and a warm smile that made his heart skip a beat.

As she left the bar, Doc looked to Jackson, his voice serious. "I'd like you to check up on her tomorrow if you don't mind. I know for a fact that no one has been up to that property in years. It might need some work."

Jackson raised an eyebrow, curious about Doc's request. "Why me?"

Doc chuckled. "Well, you're our newest resident, and it's a bit of an Aspen Cove tradition to welcome newcomers and lend a helping hand. Besides, you never know what kind of connection you might form."

"Listen to you. Stick to your day job and leave matchmaker to the grannies in the next town over," Jackson said.

Each day, Doc visited for his ritualistic tic-tac-toe match, staking his daily beer on the outcome. Jackson, aware of the game's inevitable result, preemptively filled a frosted mug for Doc. The older man never lost, ensuring his daily brew was well-earned.

"But as a neighborly gesture, you'll check on her, right?" Doc lifted the mug and took a deep drink.

How could he say no when Aspen Cove had welcomed him so warmly? He nodded. "Alright, Doc. I'll look in on her tomorrow."

Doc licked the foam from his mustache. "Good man. I have a feeling you two will get along fine."

Amanda steered her car ⟨...⟩ the winding mountain road toward her new home, the excitement bubbling inside her like champagne. The trees were dusted with fresh snow, their branches glistening, giving the landscape an ethereal glow. She could almost taste the peacefulness that awaited her.

As she rounded the final bend, Amanda's heart leaped as the cabin came into view. But the sight that greeted her was far from the picture-perfect scene she had expected. The cabin's once-sturdy wooden exterior was weathered and gray, the windows dusty and cracked, and the yard was overgrown with weeds and wildflowers. The porch sagged under the weight of neglect, and the roof looked like it had seen better days.

She blinked, trying to reconcile the reality before her with the images she had built in her mind. She had known the property might need some work, but she hadn't anticipated the extent of the disrepair. Her heart sank, and she experienced a flicker of doubt; had she made the right decision in moving to Aspen Cove?

...ation coursed through her
...had come to the small town for
...uldn't let the state of the cabin deter
...esolve, she parked her car in the gravel

...opened one eye as he lifted his head from the
...the passenger seat. He blinked at his surroundings.
...tail twitched and curled around his body like a barrier
against the outside world.

"I know it's not much now, but we can make it something," she said, her voice filled with optimism.

As if he understood her, he tucked himself into a tight ball and closed his eyes again.

"Suit yourself." She stepped out of the car and into the mountain air, shutting the door and breathing in the scent of pine. A peaceful stillness encircled her—a quietness she could never experience in the city. Leaves rustled in a soft breeze, and birds chirped, providing a soothing soundtrack to her new life.

She took in the detailed woodwork on the porch railings as she neared the cabin. Carved brambles and butterflies were proof to the care that had once gone into the home. Even in its current state, it had a certain charm, a sense of history and love embedded in its structure. Amanda sensed a connection to the place. They were both run down and left behind.

She took a deep breath and approached the entrance, her chest tight with nervousness. What mysteries awaited inside? Was it the stone fireplace she'd been dreaming of or something far less pleasant? She wasn't sure what to expect, but she knew one thing: her heart was racing.

She pushed the door open, and the hinges screeched in

protest. The interior was dim, shadows waltzing on the walls. She fumbled for the light switch, holding her breath as she flicked it on. To her surprise and relief, the lights blinked to life, showcasing what she'd inherited. Trash and debris were scattered across the floor. Cobwebs hung from the exposed wooden beams, and dirt had collected on the floorboards. The furniture lay covered in sheets, concealing the shapes within, and a stale, heavy smell permeated the air, laced with mildew and disuse.

She sighed, her shoulders drooping with the weight of disappointment. This was not the idyllic haven she had expected but rather a project requiring significant time, effort, and love to restore it to its former glory.

Despite the overwhelming dismay, she noticed the potential beneath the dust and decay. The large stone fireplace would undoubtedly provide coziness on cold winter nights. Once cleaned and replaced, the windows would offer stunning views of the surrounding landscape.

As she continued exploring the cabin, she heard a sudden rustling sound from the kitchen. Her heart rose to her throat as she stepped closer.

To her surprise and horror, an enormous raccoon peeked out from a broken cabinet. Its beady eyes focused on Amanda as it chittered, hissed, and bared its teeth, clearly unimpressed by the unexpected intruder in its makeshift home.

"Okay, okay, I get it," Amanda muttered, stepping back, and holding her hands up placatingly. "You think this place is yours." She stomped her feet, hoping to scare the critter away. In response, the raccoon lunged in her direction, and she turned and ran outside, slamming the door behind her.

Her heart boomed while she took a moment to collect

herself. This was her cabin, and she wasn't about to let a wild animal chase her away. It wasn't a bobcat or a wolf—it was a raccoon. Certainly, she could best one of those. Taking a deep breath, she steeled her resolve and marched back, determined to reclaim her new home.

Her eyes scanned the room, searching for the raccoon. With every shift of the floorboards, her heart quickened, and her senses went on high alert.

"Okay, Mr. Raccoon," she murmured, praying her soft voice would result in surrender. "I don't want any trouble. All I want is to live here in peace."

As she ventured further inside, she spotted the raccoon in the corner of the living room, its steely eyes watching her warily. She took a deep breath, trying to steady her nerves. "Hey there," she said, hoping to establish rapport with the creature. "I'm Amanda, and the cabin is my place now. I'd appreciate it if you could find somewhere else to be."

The raccoon tilted its head as if considering her words but made no move to leave. Instead, it emitted a series of chattering noises as if replying to her in its language.

She knew she couldn't let it stay but didn't want to harm it. She needed to coax it out of the space without getting too close. As she looked around, her gaze fell on a stack of old boxes piled against the wall. An idea began to form in her mind.

"Alright, Mr. Raccoon," she said, tentatively approaching. "If you don't leave willingly, I'll have to get creative."

As she reached for the top box, her hand trembling, she tried to calculate the best way to use the contents as a barrier between her and the raccoon. However, her plan went awry when she inadvertently knocked over the entire pile, sending them tumbling to the floor with a loud crash.

Amanda winced, bracing herself for the raccoon's reaction. But instead of charging her, the creature seemed stunned by the noise, its attention now focused on the mess of items that had spilled from the fallen boxes.

She took advantage of the raccoon's distraction and cautiously approached the pile. As she surveyed the scattered belongings, she realized that they were vintage Christmas decorations, their once-vibrant colors now faded with age. There were strings of old-fashioned glass balls, delicate snowflakes made from cut paper, and a pair of tarnished brass candlesticks, all nestled among the debris.

With her eyes fixed on the raccoon, she extended her hand and picked up one of the ornaments, carefully turning it over in her palm. As she explored its intricacies, a sense of wonder covered her. The ornaments served as tangible links to the cabin's past, a reminder of the previous owner who had once celebrated the holiday season in this very space. It was a poignant realization that she had now become a part of the home's history, igniting within her a renewed determination to put her own mark on the place.

She stared at the raccoon, still eyeing her from its corner. "Alright," she said, her voice firmer now. Pointing her finger toward the door, she continued, "I need you to leave. I have a lot of work to do, and I can't do it with you here."

As if in response, the critter let out another series of noises before backing away and disappearing into the shadows of the next room. Amanda released a breath she hadn't realized she'd been holding, relief flooding through her. She'd faced her fears and stood her ground, which was like a small victory in her quest for a fresh start.

With the animal out of sight, she returned to the vintage

decorations. She knew cleaning and restoring the cabin would be a monumental task, but discovering these treasures were a sign, a reminder of the magic the home once held and could hold again. As she gathered the ornaments into a box, she imagined the place transformed, filled with joy, light, and laughter.

A screech came from the raccoon's room, followed by a flurry of fur racing toward her, forcing her to retreat outside.

Exhausted and defeated, Amanda slumped against the outside doorframe, her arms crossed over her chest. She couldn't believe her first day in Aspen Cove had ended with her being bested by a raccoon.

As the sun set and the temperature dropped, she realized she couldn't stay in the cabin until she evicted the tenant. With a heavy sigh, she gathered some old quilts from the trunk of her car and decided to spend her first night in Aspen Cove sleeping in the back seat. It wasn't the inviting evening she had imagined, but it would have to do.

She wrapped herself in the covers and was serenaded by the distant howls of coyotes and the raccoon rustling inside her cabin. As she lay there, her thoughts wandered to her life back in the city, her friends, and the familiar comforts of her old apartment. She wondered if she had made the right decision to leave everything behind for a fresh start.

Nestled in the backseat of her car, Gatsby purring beside her, she pulled the quilt tighter and closed her eyes. Her thoughts shifted from the day's unforeseen hitches to the blank canvas of her new life in Aspen Cove. She conjured images of future holiday celebrations, laughter echoing through rooms she'd yet to repair. As her lips curled into a small, almost defiant smile, a newfound conviction settled in. True, Aspen Cove's welcoming ceremony had been a raccoon eviction and an unexpected night in her car. But even so, something whispered in her ear—a hint of promise, a glimmer of possibility—that sometimes the most treasured memories are born from life's little detours.

CHAPTER FOUR

As Jackson and Gunner neared Amanda's cabin, the state of disrepair struck him—untamed weeds, a weather-worn exterior, a roof in need of more than just a patch-up.

Pulling into the driveway, he saw Amanda standing there, her expression a mix of frazzle and resolve.

"Hey there," Jackson greeted, wearing a friendly smile. "Doc sent me to see how you're doing. Everything okay?"

Amanda's face seemed to lighten at his words, though a heavy undertone remained. "Well, that's kind of him, and you too, obviously. I'm managing, given the... circumstances." Her gaze shifted to the woods. "Had to resort to nature's restroom. Spent the night serenaded by wolves and owls. Wasn't sure I'd greet the morning."

Her tone made it sound like forest bathroom breaks were tantamount to life-or-death situations, offering Jackson a glimpse into the kind of night she'd had.

"Problem with the plumbing?" Gunner left his side and went to stand by her car. His ears perked up, and he growled, low and menacing.

"Hey, Buddy, what's up?"

"He probably senses Catsby."

"Catsby?"

She sighed. "It's my tabby. His full name is The Great Catsby, but that's a mouthful when calling him, so it's just Catsby."

He tapped his leg, and Gunner came back to his side. "About the plumbing. Is there an issue?"

She shrugged. "I haven't got a clue. I haven't been able to test it out. I have a squatter in the cabin."

"A what?" He knew what a squatter was but didn't understand why she was standing outside staring. "Why didn't you tell him or her to leave?"

She stood up taller. "You don't think I tried?"

"You should call the sheriff."

She let out a small, rueful laugh. "I don't think this is up his alley. It's not a person but a raccoon. A mean, beady-eyed critter that came after me."

Jackson raised an eyebrow, his curiosity piqued. "A raccoon, huh? Well, I've dealt with my fair share of critters. In fact, I've got a pretty funny story about a squirrel who managed to sneak into my tent when I was in the army, stationed in the desert. The thing stole my trail mix and had a feast on my sleeping bag while I was in it. When I woke and surprised it, it offered me a peanut with its outstretched hand before it scurried away."

Amanda laughed, and the tension in her shoulders eased. "This animal doesn't appear quite as hospitable. All he's offering me is probably rabies or the plague."

"Let's see what we're dealing with."

Jackson told Gunner to stay while he and Amanda entered. Together, they tried to locate the raccoon's hiding place. As they moved from room to room, Jackson noticed how Amanda's face would light up with excitement every time she discovered something new or interesting about the cabin. She was clearly falling in love with her home despite the mess and the unwanted visitor.

Finally, they discovered the raccoon huddled in a corner of the back bedroom, eyes wide with evident fear. Jackson sensed the animal was more frightened of them than vice versa. "Alright, little buddy. We don't want to hurt you, but you can't stay here," he said, lowering his voice to offer a calming presence. The raccoon responded with a chittering sound and bared its teeth, clearly not convinced.

Amanda jumped behind him, holding on to his jacket and peeking around to see the raccoon. "It's ridiculous. I just moved here and am already having a turf war with a local."

"What have you tried?"

"I asked it to leave. I was quite patient and nice, but it refused. Then I knocked over a box of these amazing Christmas ornaments. It simply stared and left me to them while it came into this room."

"Remember, to him, you're the uninvited guest. But don't worry, I'm here to help."

Amanda's expression softened. "I appreciate that, Jackson. I do. I hope we can get this raccoon out of my cabin, so I'm not forced to sleep another night in my car."

"Let's get to work then."

Eyeing the situation, he began to piece together a plan. "Listen, raccoons aren't just cute faces; they're sly and can turn aggressive. Those claws can slice like knives, and a bite means a tedious run-in with rabies shots."

"You speak like someone who's learned the hard way. Personal experience?"

"Sort of. A friend from my military days tried to hand-feed one some Cheetos. Ended up with a bite and a series of gut shots."

"Sounds like a lesson learned the hard way. Let's avoid bites, shall we?"

Amanda and Jackson exchanged a determined look before embarking on their first attempt to get rid of the raccoon. They had armed themselves with brooms, hoping to shoo the crafty creature out of the cabin without getting too close.

"Okay, on the count of three, we'll swing the door wide and start waving these around," Amanda whispered, her eyes wide. Jackson nodded in agreement, gripping his broom tightly.

"One... two... three!" Jackson counted, and they swung open the door, furiously brandishing their wooden weapons.

The raccoon, however, was unfazed by their efforts, tilting its head and staring at them with an almost amused expression. After several more futile attempts, Amanda and Jackson gave up, panting and laughing at their ridiculousness.

"Alright, that didn't work," Amanda admitted, wiping the sweat from her brow. "We need a new plan."

"Let's try luring it out with some food," Jackson suggested. "I've got some leftover jerky in my truck. Maybe the raccoon will go for that."

With a nod of agreement, they set up the bait right outside the door, hoping to entice the raccoon to venture out of its newfound home. Along with Gunner, they hid behind a nearby tree, watching intently for any signs of movement.

Moments later, the raccoon appeared at the doorway, cautiously sniffing the air before creeping toward the meat. As it was about to take it, Gunner bounded forward, barking, and scaring the raccoon away. It quickly retreated into the cabin, leaving Amanda and Jackson groaning in disappointment.

"Nice try, buddy," Jackson told Gunner, patting him on the head when he returned. "But we need the raccoon out of the house, not even more determined to stay inside."

Amanda sighed. "What if we create a path of noise? We could bang pots and pans, forcing it to move in our desired direction."

Jackson considered her suggestion, nodding in approval. "It's worth a shot."

They gathered a collection of noisy items from the cabin's kitchen. Positioning themselves at opposite ends of the room, they prepared to make as much of a racket as possible, hoping to drive the critter out of the cabin.

"Ready?" Jackson called. His voice was barely audible over the sound of his own racing heart.

Amanda nodded, her grip tightening on a large frying pan, causing her knuckles to turn white. "All set!"

And with that, they began their cacophonous assault, banging pots and pans, yelling, and doing everything they could to make the raccoon leave. The raccoon, however, had other ideas, managing to evade their noisy onslaught by darting back and forth between hiding spots.

Exhausted and without a backup plan, Amanda and Jackson collapsed onto the floor, their laughter echoing through the cabin. They had failed once again to rid the place of its unwanted guest.

As they caught their breath, Jackson glanced over at Amanda, an affectionate smile on his face. "We may not have succeeded, but we sure gave it our best shot."

She grinned back at him, her eyes alight with pleasure. "That we did. And who knows? Maybe the raccoon will decide to leave on its own."

Despite their unsuccessful attempts, their shared experiences created a bond between them.

They were about to give up when Gunner entered the room and took matters into his own paws. With a determined look in his eyes, he bolted into the room, his barks echoing throughout the space.

Suddenly, the raccoon darted out from its hiding spot, scampering away from the relentless pursuit of the protective shepherd. Gunner chased it through the cabin. The raccoon made a beeline for the open door, disappearing into the woods beyond.

Amanda and Jackson stared in disbelief, unable to process the sudden turn of events. Their laughter bubbled up again, this time fueled by relief and astonishment.

"Well, would you look at that," Jackson said, shaking his head. "Maybe we should've let Gunner handle it from the beginning."

Amanda nodded. "I guess sometimes the simplest solution is the best one. Good job, Gunner."

Gunner trotted back to them, his tail wagging as he received praise and affection from Amanda and Jackson.

Jackson took in the cabin's interior and noticed a window missing. "We better get that covered before he decides to come back. I imagine that's how he got in."

"Can they jump? Because that's pretty high up." She walked over and looked outside. "Oh, there's a wooden barrel right under it."

"It's like an invitation." He moved into the living room and noticed the stack of boxes. "Would you like me to cover it up? You'll need to get a glass company out here soon, but I can use some cardboard for now."

"I'd appreciate that."

Jackson went to his truck and got his toolbox. He imagined duct tape and a few nails would do. He took in the condition of the cabin again and knew Amanda would require a lot of help.

As he worked on covering the broken window, he asked, "Is the place what you were expecting?"

She looked around the room. "I'd be lying if I didn't say my fantasy was different from my reality, but with hard work, I think it can be exactly what I need."

He taped the cardboard to the frame and stepped back. "This should hold until you get someone out here."

"You're pretty handy. Do you have any experience taking a disaster and making it less so?"

"Are you trying to hire me?" He already had a job, but having twenty-four hours a day gave him lots of idle time, and he wouldn't mind working on something that filled his days.

"I hadn't considered it until this moment. I can pay, not a ton, but we can work out a deal for something fair if you're interested."

He looked around the place. "It needs a lot. The porch is about to collapse, the roof isn't in much better shape, and while the interior looks mostly cosmetic, we might find bigger problems once we look deeper."

"You're using the word we. Does that mean you're considering it?"

His eyes opened wide and shone as if the little amber flecks in them were backlit. "As it turns out, I might be." He walked down the hallway. "I see there are three rooms. What are your plans for them?"

"One will be mine, and the other an office where I'll work."

"You work from home?"

She smiled. "Yes, I'm an author."

Jackson's eyes widened with surprise. "That's pretty impressive. What kind of books do you write?"

"Romance, mostly, although recently I've been exploring other genres like women's fiction," she explained.

He nodded. "That's fascinating. I don't think I could write a book."

"It's not as easy as some people make it seem. And romance is the hardest because the story has many components. There's the hero's arc, the heroine's arc, and the story arc. Romance lovers are savvy readers and expect a central love story and an emotionally satisfying ending."

"You're speaking a foreign language to me."

"Have you ever been in love?" she asked with a smile.

Jackson shifted, averting his gaze from hers before looking back. He'd never been good at relationships. "No," he said gruffly, clearing his throat and focusing on something else in the room instead of her face.

"It can be wonderful or tragic," Amanda said.

"Sounds like you have some experience."

"Mine didn't end in a happily ever after, but I have loved, which is something."

Amanda's eyes fell on him, and they were filled with sadness. He didn't want her pity. "It's not a big deal," he said, glancing away from her and shifting uncomfortably where he stood. "I'm better at fixing things than I am at the whole relationship thing."

"And apparently I'm better at writing love stories than living them." She smiled. "Well, you have plenty to keep you busy here." She gestured around the cabin. "We should probably talk about what has to be done and how much I can pay you."

Jackson took a deep breath and walked the perimeter of the room. "The porch needs reinforcing. The roof replacing.

The windows need caulking—a lot of work needs doing here."

He explained all the needed repairs and estimated the time it would take him to do them. When he was finished, Amanda leaned against the wall and crossed her arms.

"This is going to be more expensive than I expected," she said. "I don't want to take advantage of you by offering too little money."

"I asked about the rooms because I'm in a situation. I'm staying with my buddy's brother, but they have a new baby and fear I'm in the way. It wasn't supposed to be a long-term thing. I was wondering if I could trade skills for room and board."

She stared at him like he'd grown a wart on his nose. "You want to stay in the cabin with me, and you'll work on my place for free?"

He nodded. "And food too. You'll have to pay for supplies, but I can provide the labor."

"What about Gunner? Will he eat my cat?"

Jackson laughed. "No, he prefers kibble or bacon. He also likes Katie's homemade dog biscuits."

"Are you sure? He went after that raccoon like it was his next meal."

"You want to give them a try?"

"Okay, but if he eats Catsby I won't be happy."

"Let me get him." Jackson patted his leg, and Gunner came right to him and sat.

Amanda returned with her cat, clutching him tightly to her chest. As she placed him on the kitchen counter, Gunner walked over, his nose twitching curiously.

Jackson tensed, ready to intervene, if necessary, but was surprised when Gunner sniffed at the cat without reaction.

The feline, however, was less than thrilled by the attention and hissed in response. The cat lashed out in a flash of claws and fur and sent Gunner scampering back to Jackson's side. He breathed a silent sigh of relief before glancing at Amanda, who scooped up the hissing cat. Catsby clearly had an attitude problem.

"That went well. Nobody needs stitches." She looked at Gunner once more. "When do you want to move in?"

"I can start tomorrow morning."

CHAPTER FIVE

Amanda had never before found herself so out of place as she did in that moment, standing in the middle of a long-abandoned cabin. Her new home was quaint, if not a little run down, but it had a rustic charm that was foreign and intriguing to her city-bred sensibilities. She was used to skyscrapers and the constant hum of traffic, not the whisper of wind through towering pines and the distant hooting of an owl.

When Jackson drove away, she was more alone than ever, but wasn't that what she sought—the quiet? She wondered about the person who built it and where they had stayed when they arrived. Why had they chosen this location? She couldn't argue that it was gorgeous, but what brought them here?

A thousand questions were moving in her head, but no answers, and standing there pondering them wouldn't get her any closer to moving in.

She grabbed the ends of a thick sheet draped over a worn-out armchair. The dust that had settled over the years floated in the waning rays of sunlight that seeped through the cracked window. Catsby, ever curious, jumped onto a chair, his eyes wide with interest. "Well, what do you think?" she asked, trying to keep her voice steady despite the nervous flutter in her stomach. "Could this be home?"

He blinked at her as if to say, "I'll reserve judgment until I've thoroughly inspected every nook and cranny." She chuckled, her anxiety lessening at her cat's characteristic indifference.

With the furniture now uncovered, she turned her attention to the fireplace. The chill of the night air was already seeping through the gaps in the cabin, wrapping around her like a shroud. She missed the regulated temperature of her city apartment and was painfully aware that her current attire, a pair of jeans and a short-sleeved T-shirt, wouldn't stand a chance against a frigid night.

Walking toward the hearth, she tried to recall all the information she had about building a fire. She prodded the flue with her finger, attempting to open it with no luck. She grunted in frustration as she applied more force and managed to budge it. Instead of opening up, it made a loud burping sound, and a cloud of soot came out, covering her like a blanket.

Caught off guard, she stumbled back, hacking and wheezing as the soot invaded her nose and mouth. "Oh, great." She coughed, wiping at her face only to smear the ash further. She glimpsed herself in the dusty mirror hanging above the fireplace and groaned at the sight of her streaked cheeks.

"Well, this is perfect," she said to no one in particular, her voice laced with frustration. She looked at Catsby, who was watching her with an air of bemusement from his perch on the armchair. "Don't sit there looking smug. This is your home too, you know."

The cat blinked at her, his tail flicking lazily. She sighed, deciding to let the fireplace be for the time being. Her adventure was off to a spectacularly messy start. She looked around and wondered what she had gotten herself into.

She shifted her gaze to the window, where the sun slowly sank into a melding of orange and pink hues. Its fading light illuminated the trees and cast prisms of life over the sleepy wilderness outside. The sight was breathtaking; it forced her to forget all the troubles she'd left behind and gave her hope that a new life was beyond the horizon. With one last ray of sunlight peeking between the pines, she wondered if maybe, just maybe, this little cabin would turn her life around.

With a resigned sigh, Amanda turned away from the window, her gaze landing on the fireplace again. "Well," she said, addressing the stubborn flue, "you may have won the battle, but you haven't won the war."

Catsby let out a soft warble as if in agreement, his green eyes glinting with playfulness that matched Amanda's newfound determination.

Clapping her hands together, she focused her attention on her surroundings. The cabin was small but homey, filled with old furniture that had a vintage charm. The air carried the scent of pine and dust, a weirdly comforting combination that instilled a sense of calm in her frazzled nerves.

She moved around, re-familiarizing herself with the space. The wooden floorboards protested under her weight, and every so often, a gust of wind would whistle through the cracks in the walls, sending a shiver down her spine.

Before it got too late, she raced outside to bring in the

few things she'd brought. Her clothes. Her old typewriter collection—five of her most valued possessions—bedding, food, and cleaning supplies. Anything else she needed she'd buy. A fresh start meant that she had to leave it all behind, and that's exactly what she did.

Her gaze was drawn to a small, weathered picture frame on the mantelpiece. Picking it up, she looked at a picture of a young girl, her blonde hair tied up in pigtails, grinning as she held up a fish nearly half her size. The inscription on the back read, "Brandy, Summer '96." Amanda's heart ached for the girl she once knew, her pen pal who had brought her so much joy as a child.

The cabin may have been old and needed some serious TLC, but it was also filled with remnants of a life brimming with laughter and love. It made the place feel less like a cabin and more like a home.

With a sigh, Amanda set the photo down and looked around. She was tired, sooty, and entirely out of her element, but she was here. Here in Aspen Cove, the city girl turned small-town inhabitant. The thought brought a grin to her face, one that both terrified and excited her.

Her mind wandered back to Jackson, the handsome bartender who had somehow become her future roommate. His charming smile, the way his eyes crinkled when he laughed, the comfort of his presence ... it was all so new and wonderful. She'd banned men from her life, yet a platonic friendship seemed harmless enough. Love—the part that brought pain and complications—was something she'd gladly avoid.

As night descended, the cabin grew chillier. The thermostat for the baseboard heaters was in the hallway and she crossed her fingers that they worked. Within ten minutes, the walls groaned as the timbers soaked up the heat and expanded.

She fed Catsby and found a permanent place for his litter box—the smallest room that would become her office. Tired and sore from sleeping in her car, she dreamed of a bath and walked into a bathroom with the sweetest clawfoot tub. Out of the ceiling came a showerhead she'd use tomorrow, but for now, bubbles and hot water were calling.

When she turned on the spigot, the pipes spit and sputtered before a rush of orange came out. But as quickly as it appeared, it left, and the remaining water was clear.

After thirty minutes soaking, she was pruned and ready for bed. Having almost no sleep the previous night, she was virtually snoring by the time her head hit the pillow.

In the stillness of the night, she found herself startled awake. A sudden rustling sound punctuated the eerie silence of her new cabin, reminiscent of leaves being disturbed or paper being crumpled. She froze, her heart pounding, as her mind immediately jumped to the most logical conclusion—the raccoon was back.

"Mister Raccoon, this is not a hotel," she muttered into the darkness, her voice shaky but filled with feigned bravado. It was silly talking to a raccoon as if it would understand and politely desist. However, the humor of the situation was not lost on her.

Sitting up, she strained her ears, trying to discern if the rustling was getting louder or if her imagination was playing tricks on her. The only response was the howl of a wolf somewhere in the distance.

Unable to fall back asleep, Amanda swung her legs over the side of the bed and padded across the cold wooden floor. Catsby stretched and gave her a look like she'd interrupted a dream about fish and rodents. "Don't look at me like that," she told him, "I'm making sure we don't have an uninvited guest."

Pulling her robe tighter around her, she ventured into the living room, her eyes slowly adjusting to the dim light. Her gaze fell upon a dusty old photo album tucked into the corner of a bookshelf. Curiosity piqued, she picked it up, the old leather cover cool and worn beneath her fingers.

Sitting in the old plaid chair by the fireplace, she flicked on the table lamp and opened the album, revealing pages filled with black and white photographs. They were snapshots of Aspen Cove from decades ago, showcasing its history and charm. There were images of old town gatherings, children playing in the snow, the main street decorated for the holidays, and what were likely familiar landmarks in their early years.

As she flipped through, she could almost hear the laughter, feel the chill of the winter air, and taste the homemade cookies she imagined were a staple at the town's holiday celebrations. These photos, moments frozen in time, told stories of a place that thrived on love, friendship, and the simple joys of life.

Looking at them, she had a sense of belonging. She may have been a stranger here, but in her mind, she was a friend no one had met. A soft purr drew her attention, and she found Catsby rubbing against her leg. Smiling, she reached down to scratch behind his ears. "What do you think of our new home?" He crawled into her lap and fell back to sleep.

As the night wore on, the town's atmosphere grew warmer, enfolding her in its timeless embrace.

Gradually, she transitioned from a mere observer to a living chapter in its history, as if the town itself acknowledged her presence. She imagined a distant future, a century from now, where another soul would leaf through the album she diligently curated, discovering the added photos and the stories they held.

She climbed back into bed confident the critter was still outside. The rustling and hooting no longer were strange but like a lullaby lulling her into a peaceful slumber.

A knock echoed through the stillness. Amanda stirred, her mind still foggy with dreams. A glance at the small clock on the bedside table had her groaning. "Six-thirty," she muttered to herself. "Who on earth could be visiting at this ungodly hour?"

She shuffled to the door, her hair tousled and her eyes heavy. Catsby followed closely behind, his curious eyes wide. Opening the door, she was greeted by the sight of Jackson, already wide awake, dressed in work clothes, and radiating early morning energy.

"Hello, Amanda. Hope I didn't wake you," he said far too cheerfully for this time of day. "Thought we could get started on the repairs."

Amanda blinked at him, taken aback by his drive. "It's ... it's six-thirty, Jackson," she said, emphasizing each word as if it might help convey the absurdity of the hour.

His laughter echoed through the room, causing Amanda to smile despite herself. "Well, when you said I could move in, you didn't specify working hours," he responded, grinning. "Besides, morning is the best time to get things done. Fresh air, a clear mind, chirping birds..."

He trailed off, throwing his arms out wide to indicate the dawn chorus beginning to stir. Amanda stood in her doorway, sleep-ruffled and bemused, watching him. Jackson was a picture of vitality in the soft light, his enthusiasm infectious.

He held up two Styrofoam boxes in one hand and two cups in the other. "I brought coffee and breakfast."

She moved aside to let him in. "You're forgiven for the ungodly hour, but only because I'm starving and need caffeine."

He looked down at the dog. "Can Gunner come inside?"

She smiled. "He might as well. It's going to be his home too."

As soon as Gunner entered, Catsby hissed and ran into the bedroom. She was sure he would have slammed the door behind him if he could.

"Do you think he'll get used to us?"

"He'll have to or spend much more time in our room."

Jackson brought the food to the small table in the kitchen. "I got bacon and eggs." He stopped for a second, and a frown creased his forehead. "You aren't a vegan or vegetarian, are you? If so, I can give you my hashbrowns and toast."

She shook her head. "Total carnivore here. Yesterday was hell because I only had chips, candy, and rice crispy treats. I considered stealing one of Catsby's cans of paté." She laughed. "You know you're hungry when salmon paté looks gourmet."

"I've eaten worse. Have you ever had an MRE?"

She sat and opened the box to find ample servings of eggs, bacon, potatoes, and toast. "Army food?"

"It's a stretch calling it that," he said.

She was excited to discover that he'd brought extra butter and jam. This meal was a piece of heaven. "You're the best roommate a girl could have."

He positioned himself opposite her, the wooden chair groaning as he settled into it with his large body.

"How was your first night inside?"

She thought about it and smiled. "It went well. I

thought the raccoon was back, but he didn't show his face. The heater works, but the fireplace is a mess. The hot water is good, and the bath was like a spa experience."

"I've never been to a spa."

"You should try it."

He laughed. "I might have to. I'm learning how to enjoy things once again. I've spent most of the last dozen years in unpleasant places. Being here is paradise."

"I bet that was hard." She couldn't imagine the things he'd faced as a soldier.

"It's over, and this is just beginning."

"For both of us."

The early morning chill didn't seem so bad anymore, replaced by the glow of shared laughter and conversation. As she watched Jackson, the sunlight catching in his hair, Amanda sensed a connection. Something about his easygoing nature and his unexpected kindness was drawing her in.

They finished their breakfast in silence. When she put her fork down, Jackson said, "Alright, let's get to work."

"Let me change." She looked down at her robe and realized she hadn't thought about her looks. "I'm surprised I didn't scare you away. I must look a fright."

He gazed at her for a moment. "You look amazing."

A strange flutter filled her chest, a feeling of excitement she hadn't experienced in a long time.

He lowered his head. "Sorry, I meant you look fine. You weren't expecting me at the crack of dawn." Red rose from his neck to his cheeks showing his embarrassment at complimenting her.

Not wanting to prolong it any longer, she said, "I'll be right out." She hurried into her bedroom, where Catsby lounged on her pillow. She threw on jeans and a T-shirt and slipped into her Nikes. With a quick brush of her hair and teeth, and a splash of water on her face, she was ready.

"Let's do this, Jackson." The day was beginning, and she was prepared to take on the repairs, one laughter-filled moment at a time.

As Jackson outlined the day's tasks, Amanda eagerly followed along. He spoke about fixing the cabin with such passion and care that it was impossible not to be swept up in his enthusiasm. She saw her new home through his eyes—not as a rundown disaster but as a place with history and potential—a place that could be beautiful again.

She listened intently as he guided her, his voice filled with authority. He outlined the task ahead of her—repairing the flue—step-by-step like a seasoned soldier, determined to ensure she understood every nuance of the job.

By the time they finished, the morning had given way to the afternoon. They stood side by side, admiring their handiwork. The flue was clean and functional, and a small fire crackled cheerfully in the fireplace, filling the room with a warm glow.

Watching the flickering flames, Amanda realized that this was more than a home repair project. It was about building a new life, and she wasn't alone in that. From the little she gathered from Jackson, he was also recreating himself, and they had become a part of each other's journey.

"Are you hungry? I can take you into town and introduce you to your neighbors."

Much more needed to get done, but even Rome wasn't built in a day, and the people who made it had to eat. "I think that's a solid idea, but since you bought breakfast, lunch is on me."

"Sounds like a plan." He tapped his leg, and Gunner ran to his side. "Can you stay here and be a good boy?"

Gunner barked. Jackson pointed to the corner, and Gunner walked to it and curled into a ball. "I'll meet you in the truck."

After she gathered her bag and ensured the fireplace screen was in place, she walked to the door and looked over her shoulder at Gunner. "Don't eat my cat."

CHAPTER SIX

Jackson had always been the gentlemanly type, a trait that earned him his fair share of teasing back in high school. The boys would nudge him, chuckling, "With a last name like Knight, you were destined to play the chivalrous role, weren't you?" But today, as he held his sturdy old Ford door open for Amanda, his manners transcended mere habit. It was an act that bore an undercurrent of something deeper, something that made his heart race a touch faster and his palms damp.

Each time his hand met hers, even in the briefest of touches, it was as though he could feel an energy passing between them, a silent communication that made his skin tingle.

His senses heightened when she was around. He could detect a faint flower fragrance that made him think of springtime and fresh beginnings. Her appreciative smile, and the way her eyes lit up, added an unspoken layer of connection that Jackson found himself unexpectedly responsive to. It was as if these small moments of contact were quietly weaving a bond between them, drawing him into her orbit.

His last name, Knight, had always carried a mantle of old-world courtesy and chivalry that he wore with pride, but in the presence of Amanda, it took on a higher calling. Unbeknownst to him, when Doc asked him to check on her, a newfound sense of protectiveness, the desire to make her smile, and the need to ensure her comfort surged within him. These unfamiliar yet not unwelcome feelings tugged at his heart, forging a connection that went beyond the bounds of duty.

"Your chariot awaits," he said as she approached.

She laughed. "Thank you, kind sir."

She moved to climb into the truck, her delicate hand reaching for the handle. Jackson reached out to assist her. Her hand was soft against his calloused one, but that same energy bypassed his toughened skin.

She looked up, and her warm brown eyes met his. In that fleeting moment, the world around them faded into insignificance, leaving only the magnetic pull between them. Yet, the pull of reality nudged him back to the present. He blinked, reluctantly releasing her hand, and took a step back with a sheepish smile. "Just channeling my inner 'Knight,'" he joked, attempting to dissipate the tingling sensation that coursed through his entire being, from his toes to the tips of his hair. "Chivalry seems to come bundled with the name."

Rounding the truck and climbing into the driver's seat, he put the key in the ignition and turned it, the familiar rumble of the engine offering a sense of normalcy to the unusual fluttering in his stomach. He stole a glance at her as they pulled out of the driveway.

She looked at the passing scenery, a soft smile gracing her lips. "It's so pretty."

He nodded. "It certainly is." But he wasn't talking about the forest.

Jackson refocused on the road ahead, but the memory of the spark between them lingered. They were just friends, he reminded himself. Friends and nothing more. As they drove down the road to town, he decided he would keep it that way. After all, he was there to help her settle down, not unsettle his emotions.

Jackson pulled his truck into an empty parking spot on Main Street. The small-town diner was a familiar spot, its comfort food and warm atmosphere providing a sense of homeyness he hoped Amanda would appreciate.

They stepped out of the truck, the cool air differing from the truck's heated interior. Amanda pulled her coat tighter as she followed him toward the diner's entrance. The comforting smell of burgers and brewing coffee wafted out as he held the door open for her.

"Maisey's Diner," he announced, gesturing grandly toward the bustling eatery. "Best grub in all of Aspen Cove."

She laughed. "It's the only grub, right?"

"Not true. B's Bakery and The Corner Store are here. And Dalton has a take-and-bake place in The Guild Creative Center."

"Wow, that almost compares to the offering of downtown Chicago."

"What Aspen Cove doesn't offer in amenities it makes up for in charm."

"I think you're right."

Inside, the diner was alive with chatter and the clinking of cutlery against plates. The checkered floor, vintage photos, and the warm glow from the jukebox in the corner added to the nostalgia and comfort. Jackson's favorite part was the motorcycle on display. It hung from the ceiling like it was waiting for someone to jump on and take it for a ride.

He pointed ahead. "That's Maisey."

Maisey, the diner's owner, was a woman whose personality was as vibrant as the colorful cherry-adorned apron she wore. Her eyes lit up as she spotted them, and she hurried over, her warm smile matching the twinkle in her eyes.

"Jackson! And you must be Amanda," Maisey greeted, wrapping Amanda in a friendly hug as if they'd known each other for years. "Welcome to Aspen Cove!"

Amanda looked taken aback for a moment but then relaxed into the hug, returning it with a laugh. "Thank you, Maisey. It's lovely to meet you," she replied. "Jackson has told me so much about your famous pies."

Maisey led them to an empty booth, and they took a seat. "Speaking of pies, do you want to hear a pie joke?"

"I love a good joke," Amanda said.

Maisey laughed. "Can't guarantee it's good, but here goes." She cleared her throat. "Why did the pie go to a dentist?"

Amanda shook her head. "I don't know. Why?"

"Because it needed a filling." Maisey delivered the punchline, laughing heartily at her joke. Her laugh was infectious, causing Amanda and Jackson to chuckle along.

It wasn't easy being the new kid, but Amanda was fitting in with ease. It was as if she had been a part of Aspen Cove all her life.

A peculiar sense of happiness welled up in him as she chatted animatedly with Maisey. She was curious, kind, and open.

"Shall we order?" he asked, gesturing toward the menu stuffed into the metal holder at the edge of the table. He pulled one out and handed it to Amanda. "Everything is good, but the blue-plate special is the best."

She glanced at the menu and closed it. "I'll have that."

"Don't you want to know what it is?" Maisey asked.

Amanda shook her head. "Nope. I'm happy to be surprised."

"She's a keeper, isn't she?" Maisey said, drawing his attention back to Amanda, who sat with a smile, her hands resting on her lap.

Jackson chuckled, nodding in agreement. "That she is," he replied.

Her hair was falling out of her messy bun, loose strands framing her face in a way that made her look carefree. He took in the way she gestured enthusiastically as she spoke, how her laughter filled the diner, and how she made everyone around her feel at ease. It was like watching a flower bloom in fast-forward.

"Earth to Jackson." Maisey's voice jolted him out of his thoughts. He turned to find both women looking at him.

"Sorry, lost in thought," he admitted with a grin, feeling his cheeks warm under their gaze.

"Welcome back to Earth. We've got lunch to eat. Do you want the blue plate too?" Amanda asked.

He nodded, and Maisey pivoted and left.

"Tell me about Aspen Cove," Amanda said. "I want to know everything."

Jackson laughed. "That could take a while."

Maisey zipped by, dropping off two cups of coffee, creamer, and extra napkins. Her pockets were like Mary Poppins' carpet bag. He was fairly certain that no matter what he asked for, she'd be able to produce it with a single dip into her apron.

"Well, let's start with the people. They're so friendly, so close. It's like everyone knows everyone else."

Jackson's gaze drifted over the diner. He saw Maisey at the counter, her hands flying as she chatted with a regular. A group of older men sat in a corner, their laughter echoing through the cafe. It was a sight he had grown accustomed to and loved.

"You're right," he said, turning back to Amanda. "Aspen Cove is a small town, but it's like a big family. They look out for each other. I haven't been here long—a few months—so I'm a newbie too."

"I thought you were a local."

He sipped his coffee. "I bartend, so I get to know everyone. It's the only place to hang out at night."

He went on to talk about the different families. The way she listened, leaning in, her eyes focused on him, made him feel strangely special. He wasn't a storyteller, but her attention made him want to spin tales or at least tell her all he knew.

As they continued their conversation, she asked about the town's history, celebrations, and quirks. Jackson answered as best he could, and when he didn't know something, he admitted it, promising to find out more for her or take her directly to the source so she could hear it firsthand.

Maisey dropped off meatloaf and mashed potatoes, and by the way Amanda looked at it, he would have guessed it was filet mignon and lobster. She dug in like she'd been starved for weeks. Jackson was reluctant to end their outing when they finished their meal. He was enjoying her company more than he thought possible, taking delight in the way she looked at the world, appreciating her curiosity. He wondered if she got ideas for her novels from these kinds of conversations.

After their leisurely lunch, Jackson guided Amanda to their next stop, B's Bakery. As they stepped inside, the scent of fresh-baked muffins and cookies filled the air, mingling with the soft strains of a holiday tune playing in the background.

Katie welcomed them from behind the counter, saying, "Hey y'all." She was a woman of warm smiles and laughter, a picture of contentment. As Jackson introduced Amanda, Katie's eyes lit up with genuine interest.

"I hear you're a pink letter recipient." Katie pointed to the wall behind them.

Amanda's gaze was drawn to a frame where a rose-colored letter hung among a collage of muffin-of-the-day pictures.

"What's the story with this one?" Amanda asked.

Katie's smile turned tender as she told of her experience. She had never met Bea, the previous owner of the bakery, but carried a piece of her—Bea's daughter's heart. She spoke of her arrival in Aspen Cove, lost and afraid, and how the transplant gave her a second chance at everything. The gift saved her life and offered her a new one as a proprietor, wife, and mother.

As Katie shared her story, Amanda sat there fully enthralled.

"I'm an author, but this is better than anything I could make up."

Katie beamed. "We have another writer in town. Her name is Reese. You'll have to meet her."

"I'd love that."

"First things first, though. The first treat is on the house. What will it be?"

Amanda moved up and down the display case as if staring at the crown jewels.

"I can't choose. Surprise me."

"Today is raspberry muffin day. They're the sheriff's favorite."

"I never argue with the law. Raspberry muffin it is."

Katie came around the counter with a plate with two muffins and led them toward a wall filled with hundreds of pieces of paper. "The Wishing Wall is a tradition here," Katie explained. "People write their wishes on sticky notes and put them there. We believe it carries our desires to the universe. I grant the simple ones; the others I must leave for God."

Amanda seemed moved by the custom. Her eyes scanned the wall, taking in the wants and needs of many, some uncomplicated like a dozen cookies and others more profound like a cure for cancer. It was a snapshot of the town's hopes and dreams. Jackson was touched by the raw honesty and vulnerability they represented.

With an encouraging smile, Katie offered them each a sticky note. "Would you like to make a wish?" she asked.

Jackson hesitated, but he joined in, seeing Amanda's excitement. As he scribbled, he stole a glance at her. She was deep in thought, her brows knitted together. She picked up a pen and began writing, and he found himself hoping, more than anything, that her wish would come true.

Amanda finished and smiled as she stuck her note to the wall. Her eyes shone with happiness, and Jackson grinned back. He folded his in half put his wish right next to hers.

"Are you going to tell me what you wished for?" she asked as they walked away.

"Nope," Jackson replied, grinning. "I imagine sharing your wish before it comes true is bad luck."

She rolled her eyes playfully. "Fine, keep your secrets."

They said their goodbyes to Katie, with Amanda

inviting her to the cabin for a visit. He opened the bakery door and led them out. The sun began to dip behind the mountains, casting a golden glow over the small town. Snowflakes hung in the air, catching the light, and making the scene magical.

"If it's going to snow, it would be wise to pick up supplies. Unless you're okay with eating rice crispy treats and Fancy Feast," Amanda said.

"I'm pretty easygoing when it comes to food."

She laughed. "You'd have to fight Catsby for it. He's not much into sharing, so I imagine we should stock up on what we need." She pointed to The Corner Store. "I can make it quick if you have plans."

"Nothing planned except moving into my room. I'm not working at the bar tonight, so I'm all yours."

Was that a blush he saw creeping from her neck to her cheeks? Maybe he wasn't the only one feeling the connection.

CHAPTER SEVEN

She tipped her face to the sky, closed her eyes, and allowed the chilly flakes to dust her skin. A delighted giggle bubbled from her lips, her breath misting in the cold air. It was serene, and utterly amazing.

"In Chicago, this comes with gale-force winds." She stopped in the middle of the street. "Listen. It's so quiet, you can almost hear the snowfall." That was the one thing she absolutely loved about her new home. In the silence, she noticed everything.

She turned to share her joy with Jackson and found him absorbed in something on his phone. His brows lifted, and his lips tugged into a thin line. The cheerful man she had been laughing with a moment ago was replaced with this serious, stern-looking one. The sudden change in his demeanor sent a jolt of worry through her.

"The weather report just updated, and the storm is going to be worse than expected," he said, his voice cutting through her thoughts. He showed her his screen.

Amanda glanced at it, her eyes widening as she took in the swirling mass of white and blue on the weather app.

"How much snow are we talking about?" Her heart pounded. She was a city girl through and through. She had experienced heavy snowfall in Chicago, but street plows and city workers always followed it to clear it up. She had no idea what to expect from a snowstorm in Aspen Cove. She swallowed hard, forcing herself to meet Jackson's gaze. "Is it ... is it going to be bad?"

"It's likely to be a sizable one," he revealed. "It says six to ten inches." His gaze never left her face. "But don't worry, we'll be prepared."

She nodded, her throat feeling tight. She could very well be stuck in her cabin with Jackson for days. She hardly knew him, but her gut told her he was a good person. Surely, Doc wouldn't send someone to look after her that wasn't trustworthy. Then again, she didn't know Doc. Her inner voice reminded her that she'd invited him to live with her the day after she met him. That behavior was unusual for her, but in his presence, she experienced a newfound sense of goodness. From that moment onwards, her perception of him had only grown more positive. He consistently demonstrated kindness and generosity, leaving her with an undeniable feeling of goodwill and trust.

"Let's get stocked up," she said. They agreed that she'd provide room and board, and she wasn't about to go back on her word. "Oh my, I don't even know if the stove and refrigerator work."

"They do. I checked them this morning when you went to shower. Everything is functional."

"Thank the Lord."

As they walked, storefronts with their Christmas lights twinkled merrily, the smell of mouth-watering brownies from the bakery hung in the air, and the soft hum of carols sounded in the distance. It was a picture-perfect postcard scene, contradicting the storm that was brewing.

"They sure start Christmas early here. We haven't even gotten to Thanksgiving." She hadn't considered the day generally celebrated en masse by families all over the United States. It was only two weeks away. She wondered where she'd be. Would she share it with Jackson or eat a turkey TV dinner with Catsby?

"I think Katie is leading the holiday decor charge, but I also imagine it gets pretty chilly to be out decorating in the snow."

"Right." She hadn't considered that, but it sounded wise not to hang lights or paint windows in a blizzard.

As they approached the store, Amanda marveled at the scene artfully painted across the glass. An idyllic, snowy landscape unfurled in frosted pastels, dotted with quaint cottages that emanated a sense of coziness and festivity. Each house was painstakingly detailed, smoke wafting from miniature chimneys and each window twinkling as if lit from within.

A jolly Santa Claus with rosy cheeks and twinkling eyes took center stage astride his sleigh piled high with fancy wrapped gifts. His strong and graceful reindeer were captured mid-leap, creating the illusion of movement as if flying across the winter sky. Santa's hearty laugh was almost audible, the artist skillfully capturing the infectious joy and spirit of the season.

Beside Santa, a majestic Christmas tree stood tall, its branches heavy with glistening snow. It was adorned with multicolored baubles, twinkling lights, and strands of shiny tinsel, a star perched on top, standing out against the painted night sky.

The edges of the window held delicate snowflakes, each

unique and precisely designed. Their icy, crystalline patterns sparkled as they caught the light, creating a stunning frame for the festive scene within.

"That is gorgeous. It must have cost a fortune."

Jackson laughed. "That's not how the town works. The artist is a local, Sosie Grant, who volunteered her talents. Most of the paintings you'll see in town are hers."

"Well, she's amazing."

Jackson opened the door to let her inside, and The Corner Store, with its homely charm, reminded Amanda of an old country market. Baskets filled with fresh fruits and vegetables sat inside the entrance; buckets of flowers sat near the register as if waiting to hitch a ride home in someone's cart.

Despite the charming, laidback esthetic, the store was abuzz with urgency. In their haste to gather supplies, the townsfolk transformed what was probably a quiet store into a bustling marketplace.

Navigating through the narrow aisles, Amanda found herself clinging to Jackson, her senses overwhelmed. The store was a symphony of sounds – the rustle of paper bags, the soft chime of the cash register, the murmur of conversation. The intimate setting transported her to a world far removed from the spacious, sterile supermarkets she had grown accustomed to in the city.

Jackson's presence, however, was a calming force in the whirlwind of activity. His easy familiarity with the store and its patrons and calm demeanor eased her anxiety.

The approaching storm had brought the town together in a way Amanda hadn't anticipated. As they prepared to weather the snowstorm, she could only marvel at the sense of closeness—a stark contrast to city life's impersonal hustle and bustle.

Amanda's gaze was drawn to a whirlwind of motion near the canned goods. A woman, her hair knotted up in a messy bun with a baby perched on her hip, was herding a group of children of varying ages. Despite the apparent chaos, the woman was unfazed, navigating the small store with awe-inspiring ease.

"Who's that?" Amanda asked Jackson, nodding subtly toward the spectacle.

"That's Louise," Jackson answered, following Amanda's gaze. "And those are her eight kids. Believe it or not, she's always the picture of calm in the storm."

Amanda watched as Louise ushered her brood down the aisle, her voice firm but kind as she instructed the older ones to help the younger ones. The children, for all their energy, listened to their mother, their actions reflecting respect and adoration for the woman who guided them.

The scene left an incredible heartwarming impression, enveloping Amanda with a deep sense of familial love. As she witnessed Louise's interactions with her children, a pang of longing surged within her, sparking a yearning for her own family. However, she swiftly quashed the thought, resolute in her decision that the only love she would embrace would be the one she expressed through her written words and stories.

"Must be a handful," Amanda commented, her voice soft as she continued to watch the family.

"She and her husband, Bobby, take it all in stride. Doc often says that if Louise didn't stop at eight, Bobby would have had them populate the town of Aspen Cove on their own."

As they continued shopping, Amanda found herself stealing glances at Louise as she maneuvered her large brood, shepherding them with the practiced ease of a seasoned conductor leading an eager orchestra. The children, in return, moved with a chaotic harmony, their energy both infectious and overwhelming.

Jackson rushed forward when one of the eight sat on the ground and screamed. "Need a hand, Louise?" Louise looked over, her eyes brightening at the sight of Jackson. "I can always use an extra set of hands."

Jackson turned to Amanda, winking conspiratorially. "Ready to dive into the deep end?"

A thrill of nervous excitement fluttered in her chest, but she nodded, her competitive spirit piqued. "I think I can handle it."

The next half hour was a whirlwind of activity. Amanda and Jackson found themselves in the thick of Louise's bustling family, helping to corral children, fetch items from high shelves, and keep an eye on the wandering toddler who was determined to explore every nook and cranny.

Amid the bustling store, Amanda found herself laughing more freely than she had in ages. The children were endearing, peppering the air with questions that tickled her funny bone. "Where do eggs come from?" one asked, only to follow up with, "Then where do chickens come from?" Jackson, usually so reserved, seemed to thrive in the chaos, his guard down as he joined in the banter and childlike curiosity.

At one point, Amanda looked over at Jackson, huddled with two of Louise's boys, their heads together as they debated which brand of hot chocolate was the best. Jackson was animated, his expression brimming with laughter as he listened to the boys' passionate arguments. The sight of him, so at ease and engaged, sent tingles spreading through Amanda's chest.

"The kind you make from scratch," she said, watching as they took two boxes of Swiss Miss from the shelf.

By the time they finished helping Louise and her children, Amanda realized the chaos, rather than draining her, had filled her with energy.

As they waved goodbye to Louise and her family, the store was too quiet, the absence of the children's laughter echoing in her ears.

"Let's finish and get out of here," Jackson said.

She looked out the window and realized that several inches of snow had fallen in the time they'd spent helping Louise.

Amanda became increasingly aware of Jackson's preferences as they moved through the aisles at lightning speed. It began as small, seemingly insignificant observations—how his hand lingered on a particular brand of coffee and his eyes lit up at the sight of a specific type of cereal. As they continued, however, she realized that their tastes were strikingly similar.

Jackson turned to her at one point, holding up a jar of homemade apple butter. "Have you ever tried this?"

Amanda shook her head, her curiosity piqued. "No, I can't say I have."

"Ah, you're missing out. It's fantastic on toast." He placed the jar in their basket, throwing her a look that promised a shared experience in the future.

As they continued their shopping, conversation flowed easily between them. They talked about their favorite meals, the comfort foods that reminded them of home. Amanda was surprised to learn that Jackson loved to cook, a hobby they both shared.

"I make a mean lasagna," Jackson confessed, his eyes filled with a hint of competitiveness.

"My baked ziti will beat your lasagna any day."

"Is that a challenge, Ms. Anderson?" Jackson countered, grinning at her.

"Consider the gauntlet thrown, Mr. Knight," Amanda said, her smirk perfectly mirroring his. They sealed the agreement with a handshake, and a surge of excitement coursed through Amanda, filling her with a thrilling sense of anticipation.

They picked up the ingredients they needed for their respective dishes, their conversation light and filled with laughter.

He tried to pay at the register, but she reminded him that the deal was room and board in exchange for labor.

As they left the store, their shopping bags filled with ingredients and supplies for the impending storm, her competitive side engaged. They had unwittingly set up a cooking challenge, a promise of shared moments and culinary exploration. She was looking forward to learning more about Jackson and peeling back the layers of his character, one meal at a time.

As they began the journey back to Amanda's cabin, the heavy snowfall muffled the world around them. She loved the quiet serenity of the snow-covered streets, the way the fairy lights twinkled in the snowy night, and the comfort of Jackson's presence.

As they pulled into the cabin's driveway, Amanda smiled at Gunner pressing his nose against the window. It was as if he had awaited their return, anxiously watching the world outside.

"Look at him," Amanda laughed, pointing out Gunner to Jackson. "I swear, he's like a little kid waiting for Santa."

Jackson chuckled, his gaze following hers to the window

where Gunner was now bouncing up and down. "He's excited to see us."

"I hope he didn't eat my cat."

Jackson laughed. "Your cat is more likely to eat Gunner, and he seems fine."

Once they were inside, Gunner's excitement was palpable. He jumped around, his tongue lolling out of his mouth, his tail wagging so hard that it propelled him around the room. It was a joyous welcome home.

Catsby, on the other hand, meandered into the kitchen and gave her a look that said, "I've been sleeping for fifteen hours, and I'm starved."

"Coming right up." She opened a can of Fancy Feast and set it on the old sideboard. Catsby could care less that Gunner was equally interested in a meal. He gave the dog a you-are-an-inferior-species look and started eating.

Jackson came in with another armload of groceries and said, "This is it. I think I'll feed Gunner and then try to shore up the porch with a 2 x 4 I have in the truck. With the weight of this snowfall, I want to make sure it doesn't completely collapse."

He fed the dog and excused himself. She admired how he moved with purpose, his muscles flexing under his shirt as he carried the heavy piece of wood. He was strong, capable, and reliable—all good qualities in a man.

While Jackson was outside working on the porch, Amanda busied herself with putting away the groceries. She took her time organizing the pantry and the fridge.

As she worked, she found her thoughts drifting back to Jackson. She thought about his gentle nature, his kindness, his strength. She considered how he had supported Louise and her children at the store, assured her about the oncoming storm, and reinforced her porch without even being asked.

She grabbed her phone. She had one bar despite the mountain location and her lack of internet service. A call would never go through but a text ... maybe.

Meg, I'm here, and you won't believe what's happened.

The dots moved across her screen, and Meg's message appeared.

You are in so much trouble, young lady. I've called a dozen times. I was ready to send out a search team. Are you okay?

She was better than okay.

I'm in the cabin. It's a beautiful disaster. There was a raccoon, and now there's a snowstorm. I may be trapped here for days.

The dots appeared again.

I've got a spare bedroom if you want to come here.

She loved Meg, but Florida wasn't for her.

You have hurricanes, and humidity. And Florida doesn't have Jackson.

She waited for all of two seconds before Meg responded in all caps.

WAIT. WHO IS JACKSON?

Amanda laughed.

He's my handyman, my roommate, and, maybe, my muse.

Almost a minute passed before Meg replied.

I need all the deets.

She looked out the window at Jackson, who was still

working on the porch. His forehead crinkled in concentration, his muscles flexing with each swing of his hammer.

No time now. I've got to go, but I'll call you when I can. It will probably be a few days.

She set her phone down and decided to make hot chocolate. She took out the cocoa powder, the sugar, and the milk, put them in a pot, and began to heat them on the stove. The rich, chocolatey scent filled the cabin.

Jackson walked inside as she poured the hot cocoa into two mugs. He saw her standing there and smiled.

"You know what's perfect with hot cocoa?"

She could think of a thousand things, like marshmallows and fresh cookies, but something in his eyes told her she'd be wrong.

"Tell me."

"A fire," he exclaimed, nonchalantly shrugging off his jacket and draping it on the hook beside the door. Jackson moved through her cabin with a familiarity that suggested he belonged there, as if it were his own. Or perhaps it was the undeniable truth that he embodied a sense of home for her.

CHAPTER EIGHT

He headed for the fireplace, determined to get a blazing fire started. The baseboard heaters did their job, but nothing was as inviting as a fire. Pulling off his gloves, he crouched down, reaching for the neatly stacked logs on the hearth. He chose two, their surfaces smooth and dry under his fingertips, evidence of careful chopping and storage.

Jackson laid the logs in the grate, mindful of the architecture of the fire. This wasn't about heat. Building a fire was an art, a balance of fuel, oxygen, and heat, each element crucial to the next. His father had taught him this during their camping trips in the wilderness. Those lessons, imbued with patience and respect for nature, had stuck with him. Lessons he wished he could do over again to spend more time with his father, who'd passed several years ago. His mom had left the world the year before that. He was basically an orphan looking for a place to belong. That's why he loved Aspen Cove. It was where he could become a part of something bigger than himself. He desperately wanted to belong.

Near the logs, he placed a few pieces of kindling—dry,

thin sticks that would catch fire quickly. A ball of crumpled newspaper from his pocket served as a final touch. The paper would burn rapidly, transferring heat to the kindling and igniting the larger logs. His father used to say this was the foundation of a long-lasting, warming fire.

With a strike of a match, the fire was born. It started small, the timid flames consuming the newspaper and licking at the kindling. The orange glow brightened, casting flickering shadows around the cabin's interior. He added another log, his eyes focused on the flames, their hypnotic sway a reflection of raw, elemental power.

Gradually, the flames grew bolder, the kindling crackled and popped, and the logs caught fire. The bright, warm flames spread, their incandescent glow illuminating the cabin, painting the walls in shades of amber and gold. The smell of burning wood and the soothing crackling sound filled the room, cocooning the space in an embrace of rustic charm.

As the fire blazed, Jackson sat back on his heels, a sense of satisfaction settling within him. The fire was more than a source of heat; it was a connection to his past, his father's lessons, and the simpler times. With its heat and light, the fire in the hearth was now part of his present and the shared experience with Amanda in this humble cabin. The flames cracked and hissed, and he knew this fire, like his growing bond with Amanda, would be tended to while they were in Aspen Cove for winter.

She handed him a cup of cocoa, and he joined her on the couch. They sat silently, watching the fire.

"Do you miss it?" Jackson asked, breaking the silence. His voice was soft, his gaze fixed on the hearth. "The life you left behind?"

Amanda was silent for a moment. "I miss some things,"

she admitted, her voice just above a whisper. "But not the things that matter. Not the things that make life worth living."

Jackson turned to look at her, his gaze searching her face. "What do you mean?" he asked.

Amanda took a deep breath. "I miss the local cafe where I got my coffee every morning. I miss the bagel shop on the corner that baked my favorite cinnamon crunch on Wednesdays. I miss many things, but one thing I don't miss is the memories of my ex..." she said, her voice trembling. "He made me believe I wasn't worth loving, or I wasn't enough. I let his words, his actions, freeze me in place. I stopped living, stopped experiencing things. And then he abandoned me." She paused for a few breaths. "But now..." she said, a small smile tugging at the corners of her lips. "Now, I feel free. Free to experience everything life has to offer. Free to be me, without fear of judgment, without fear of not being enough because I am enough." She made a pfft sound. "I was certainly enough when I was supporting both of us while he figured out what he wanted to be."

Jackson was silent for a moment, his gaze never leaving her face. Then, he reached out, taking her hand in his.

"I'm glad you're here, Amanda," he said. "I'm glad you're free."

"Me too."

Jackson was pulled out of his thoughts by the sound of Catsby leaping onto the couch beside him, followed by an audible thump. The large tabby uncurled himself and stretched out before settling down contentedly against Jackson's side, a deep rumble of pleasure emanating from its chest. He let out a low chuckle, slowly moving one hand to lightly scratch behind the cat's ears. The movement prompted another louder purr in response.

From where he was positioned on the other side of Amanda, Gunner huffed, his eyes half-closed but his tail wagging. Jackson smiled at the sight. Despite the howling wind and swirling snow outside, inside the little cabin was a scene of absolute serenity.

"You know," he said, looking down at Catsby and then to Gunner, "I never thought I'd be a cat guy. Or a dog guy, for that matter. I always figured they were too much responsibility, too much fuss. But I've got to say that something about a wagging tail or a purring ball of fur makes everything else insignificant."

Amanda smiled, reaching over to give Gunner a soft pat. "They have a way of doing that, don't they?" She glanced over at Jackson, her gaze soft. "I never imagined I'd be here, in a cabin, with three wonderful companions and a fire to keep me warm. But now that I am, I wouldn't trade it for anything."

The conversation subsided, giving way to the soothing crackle of the fire and the hushed embrace of the snowstorm outside. In the silence, Jackson experienced an uncommon ease, as if the absence of words echoed his deep contentment. He had grown accustomed to such stillness, even yearned for it, but seldom found it in the presence of others. Thoughts of Sage, Cannon, and their baby crossed his mind, leading him to realize that perhaps he wasn't the source of the feeling of being unsettled. If he were to be honest with himself, the inn was filled with constant busyness that made it hard for him to truly unwind. This moment, right here, was perfection—a sanctuary of peace within the chaos.

"You know," he began, breaking the quiet with his low voice. "I've always been fond of the quiet." He spoke the words as though they were a confession, an intimate secret shared between them.

Amanda turned to him, her eyes bright and attentive. "Really?" she asked, her surprise genuine.

He let go of her hand and rose, then picked up his backpack from the corner before retaking a seat. He slipped his hand inside and pulled out a leather-bound book. It was a copy of Ernest Hemingway's *For Whom the Bell Tolls*, the edges of its pages browned with age, its spine creased from multiple reads.

"Yes, it's ... peaceful. A moment to be with my thoughts. And a chance to lose myself in a good book."

Amanda reached out, her fingers brushing over the book's cover. "You're reading Hemingway?"

"Guilty," he admitted with a self-deprecating smile.

She appeared genuinely surprised, her eyes wide, but not in a way that suggested disbelief or mockery. Instead, it was as if she saw him in a new light.

"That's ... I wouldn't have expected that," she admitted.

"What did you expect?" he asked.

A charming shade of pink bloomed on her cheeks. "I don't know ... A cowboy book or maybe Jack Reacher. With your army background, maybe some Patterson, Coben or Baldacci."

He laughed a deep sound that echoed in the small space. "Well, I have a few of those authors in my collection, but I love the classics."

Amusement replaced the surprise in her gaze. "Well, I stand corrected." She pointed to several boxes stacked against a wall. "I have a collection of typewriters. One is purported to have been used by Hemingway, but I suspect it's the brand he liked and not his actual typewriter. Either way, I love it."

"Do you type on it?"

She gasped. "Never. Could you imagine? There's no

easy way to correct mistakes. I'd go through a forest of paper for a first draft."

"Modern technology is a bane and a boon."

She turned to him. "So, what else do you read?" she asked, tucking a stray strand of hair behind her ear. Her hand went back and gripped her mug of cocoa.

"Well, I read a bit of everything. A good story is a good story, no matter the genre," he said, a shrug playing at his broad shoulders. His eyes were drawn to her hands, how she cradled the mug, the color of her nails—a soft pink—providing a subtle contrast against the white ceramic.

"Any favorite author?" she pressed, her gaze expectant.

The question was simple, yet it sent him down a memory lane he rarely traversed. He considered his response, his mind weaving through the various authors and stories he'd read over the years. "Don't judge me, but I love Diana Gabaldon."

Amanda blinked, taking a moment to process his response. Then, she broke into a laugh, her eyes filled with a mixture of surprise and delight. "I didn't see that coming. But I'm starting to realize there's a lot about you I didn't see coming."

There was something in her words, in her gaze, that sent a warm thrill through him. He was used to being overlooked and people making assumptions about him based on his appearance and occupation. But she was looking at him, really seeing him. And it brought him great joy.

"Why Gabaldon?" she asked, leaning toward him.

"I suppose ... her characters. They're raw, real, flawed." He paused, trying to gather his thoughts into something coherent. "They endure, despite the odds. There's a certain nobility in that, don't you think?"

She looked at him. "I love Outlander too, but probably

because of Jamie Frazier, whereas you probably like the historical part."

"I like the whole concept of two worlds colliding." He sipped his cocoa. "Your turn," he prompted. "Who's your favorite author?"

Her eyes widened as if surprised by his interest. She nibbled on her lower lip as seemed to deliberate. "Jane Austen," she confessed.

Her answer surprised him. He expected someone like Nora Roberts, Yet, thinking about it, it also made sense. The classics, like Austen, were known for their engaging narratives, complex characters, and insightful social commentary. "*Pride and Prejudice?*" he asked with a lift to his brow.

She laughed then, a warm, genuine sound that bounced around the cabin and burrowed deep into his chest. "Predictable, right?" She rolled her eyes. "But yes, *Pride and Prejudice*. When I grow up, I want to be Elizabeth Bennett."

"Who knew?" An unexpected sense of camaraderie overtook him. It was remarkable how quickly they'd found common ground, how easily their conversation flowed. It was refreshing how she spoke about her passions and how her eyes lit up when she delved into a subject she cared about.

The hours slipped by unnoticed as the conversation flowed naturally between them, the two of them drawn together by the shared comfort of their favorite stories.

They snacked on a frozen pizza, but the conversation never stopped.

His curiosity guided him. He observed Amanda, studying her reactions, wanting to tread carefully so he didn't offend but he wanted ... no, needed to know more.

"You don't seem the type to pack up your entire life on a

whim, are you?" A smile tugged at his lips to lighten the seriousness of his question.

She shook her head. "No, I'm not."

A series of emotions flickered across her face. There was a mix of nostalgia, melancholy, and a touch of regret, quickly replaced by a steely resolve that he'd grown to associate with her.

"I needed something different to get me out of the funk I was in, so I asked for a sign, and it came the next day. I'm not one to test fate."

Jackson knew all about the desire for a fresh start. The feeling of being stuck in a rut, of wanting something different ... something more. His gaze softened as he leaned back, tucking an ankle over his knee.

"I can understand wanting to escape the noise, the rush. Aspen Cove's the perfect place for that."

Her eyes met his, and he saw a flash of understanding there. "It's peaceful," she agreed. "A perfect place for a new beginning."

He appreciated the small town's serenity but hadn't considered what it could offer to someone like Amanda. To her, this town wasn't just a quiet place to live, it was a sanctuary, a place to heal and start anew.

He admired her for her bravery to uproot her life for something better. A strong urge coursed through him, compelling him to provide reassurance, to convey that she had indeed made the right choice. That Aspen Cove, with all its quirks and charm, would be the home she needed it to be.

"What I love about living here is that we look out for one another," he assured her. "You're part of the community now. You'll never be alone."

A sudden urge to lighten the atmosphere overtook him.

Nudging Gunner with his foot, he directed the dog's attention to Catsby, who was leisurely sprawled on the rug before the fireplace.

"Watch this," he whispered. Gunner, following Jackson's prompt, began to inch closer to Catsby, nudging the cat with his nose. Catsby, in return, swatted Gunner, causing the dog to back away, only to try again. After a few times, Catsby gave in, and Gunner settled in next to the cat. The two fell asleep and snuggled up to each other.

"Yesterday, I would have never thought that possible," she said.

He finished his cocoa and put the empty mug on the coffee table. "It's amazing the difference a day can make."

"When I first read that letter... it was like a lifeline," she confessed, delicately tracing the rim of her mug. "There was this rush of hope and excitement, something that hadn't stirred within me in a very, very long time."

"You were fearless," he found himself saying. "Not everyone dares to take such a leap of faith."

Her eyes met his. "You can't do the same thing and expect something different to happen."

Her words rang true. "They say the journey of a thousand miles begins with a single step."

"You quote philosophers too. I'm impressed."

"Oh, don't be. I had a lot of free time and did a good deal of reading."

"I get that, but while you're reading Lao Tzu and Hemingway, I bet your fellow soldiers are reading *Playboy* and the Sunday comics."

He chuckled. "You're probably right." With a reluctant sigh, Jackson rose. "I guess it's getting late. I should start setting up my room." The fire was dying down, the cabin was falling into a peaceful quiet, the animals were asleep, and Jackson was standing at the edge of an emotional precipice, staring down at a swirling vortex of feelings for Amanda.

But tonight, he decided, was about understanding, and supporting her. Tonight, was about acknowledging her courage and her journey. It was about respecting her and the emotional catharsis she'd been through.

As he retired to his room, he knew their friendship was evolving into something deeper—something he hadn't expected.

As he lay down on his bed, the snow beating against the cardboard-covered window, he thought about the evening they had shared, and it struck him as funny. How did a rundown cabin, a cup of cocoa, a frozen pizza, and a fire become the highlight of his year? It was because it all included Amanda.

CHAPTER NINE

Amanda stirred from a peaceful slumber, her eyelashes fluttering open to reveal a world bathed in soft, otherworldly light. Blinking away the remnants of sleep, she pushed herself to sit up, her gaze drawn toward the window. A breathtaking view met her eyes. The cabin and surrounding landscape were wrapped in a pristine blanket of snow.

The once-familiar scene had transformed overnight into a glittering winter wonderland, every inch of it glowing under the tender caress of the morning sun. Icicles hung like delicate chandeliers from the cabin's eaves, the bare branches of the trees around her were adorned with puffs of white, and the ground was a canvas of untouched brilliance.

It was so quiet, so peacefully serene. Time had slowed, holding its breath in the face of such extraordinary beauty. Amanda's heart filled with awe and warmed her from the inside. She was witnessing a secret part of Aspen Cove, a silent poetry that unfolded with each season.

She padded toward the window in her flannel pajamas and bare feet on the cool wooden floor, her breath fogging up the glass as she took in the beauty. She pressed her palms against the cool surface, a content sigh escaping her lips. In that moment, the world appeared rejuvenated, clean, and full of promise despite, or perhaps because of, the storm.

The tantalizing tang of coffee and something deliciously warm and buttery wafted up to her from the kitchen, tearing her attention away from the view. Amanda's stomach gave an appreciative rumble, and she headed down the hallway, drawn by the scent and muffled movement sounds.

Jackson was in the kitchen, his back to her, focused on the sizzling pan before him. She was met with a comforting domestic scene: steam rising from the coffee pot, the light clinking of cutlery, and Jackson, big and solid, donning an apron that she knew said, "Domestic Goddess in Training."

Surprise and a dash of affection swelled within her. She'd known Jackson was considerate, but this scene added a layer to him that she hadn't expected, something touchingly mundane yet utterly endearing.

"Good morning," she greeted, leaning against the doorway. Jackson turned at her voice, a boyish grin lighting up his face and reaching his eyes as he flipped a pancake.

"Morning, sleepyhead," he teased, a playful glint in his eyes. "Hope you're hungry."

Her heart fluttered at his easy, charming smile. Despite the chill outside, the cabin was comfortable, filled with the sounds of a crackling fire, the delicious hint of breakfast, and the presence of a newfound friend.

She sat at the small kitchen table, while Jackson crept around the kitchen. He hummed a soft tune under his breath.

As they settled into breakfast, Jackson said, "Cannon and Sage will swing by with their truck soon. They offered to plow the driveway and make sure the road is clear. That way, I can make it to my shift at the bar tonight."

Amanda paused mid-bite, her forkful of fluffy pancake hanging in mid-air. She looked up at Jackson, curiosity clear on her face. "Do they do that for everyone around here?" she asked. The idea of such care and camaraderie in a town was foreign to her.

Jackson chuckled, his eyes crinkling at the corners as he nodded. "Not everyone, but those of us who live a bit further out, yes. That's how it is in Aspen Cove."

His obvious affection for the town and its people struck a chord within her. Here there was the sense of belonging and being a part of something that cared for you as much as you cared for it. She was a stranger—an outsider—but she didn't feel that way.

She took in Jackson's relaxed posture, the satisfied smile on his face, the ease in his demeanor. He was someone firmly grounded in his environment, someone who appreciated the importance of social ties and togetherness, and it was clear that he was a valued part of this town.

The sound of a vehicle crawling through the snow reached them. Jackson rose, a quick "excuse me" tossed over his shoulder as he grabbed his jacket from the hook and headed outside.

For the longest time, she had been adrift, lost in a sea of unfamiliar faces and unfulfilling surroundings. She had been searching for something real, substantial, and meaningful. Watching Jackson stride out to greet their visitors, a crazy thought occurred to her—maybe, just maybe, she had found it.

She moved to the window, her fingers tracing the frosty pattern on the glass as the plow maneuvered its way up their driveway.

At this moment, she was struck by a profound realization. She was not an observer here, not a transient character passing through. She was becoming a part of this wonderfully welcoming town.

An overwhelming sense of happiness covered her, flooding her heart with joy. She was indebted to Bea for guiding her to this place, appreciative of Jackson for his unwavering kindness, and thankful for the warm embrace of Aspen Cove, which had welcomed her with open arms.

The truck made its way down the drive, clearing the path and ensuring that life in this corner of the world continued, unfettered by the snow. She made a silent promise to herself and this town. She would become a part of this place, contribute to its charm and be there for others as they were there for her.

She hurried into her room to dress and returned to the living room just as Jackson ushered Cannon and Sage inside.

"Amanda, this is Cannon and his wife, Sage," Jackson introduced, a hint of satisfaction in his voice as if showing off his friends. Amanda greeted them warmly, especially Sage. After all, she had heard a little about Sage from Katie, her curiosity piqued by the woman who had made such a significant journey in life.

The conversation flowed easily, with the introductions out of the way and cups of hot coffee warming their hands. Amanda found herself drawn to Sage. And so, she found herself asking, "Sage, I heard from Katie that you used to be Bea's palliative care nurse. What made you decide to come to Aspen Cove?"

Sage looked surprised. Her face softened into a reminiscent smile. "Bea," she said, her voice warm with affection for the woman they all held dear. "She had this knack for understanding people, for seeing what they needed even when they didn't realize it themselves."

Amanda listened as Sage unraveled her tale. She shared about her time in Denver, about the soul-draining routine she was stuck in, and the unhappiness that had clung to her like a second skin. She talked about Bea and the pink envelope that had been her ticket to a new life.

"She left me the envelope and asked my supervisor to fire me," Sage said, chuckling at the memory. "I remember being shocked and hurt. But when I read her letter, it all made sense. She knew I wasn't happy and wanted me to find a place where I could be."

The transformation of Sage's life after moving to Aspen Cove was nothing short of extraordinary. She spoke of her work as a nurse with Doc Parker, a job she loved and appreciated. She talked about her marriage, her child, and the happiness that filled her life. Her story was a tribute to the power of taking chances and the magic of Aspen Cove.

Amanda found herself hanging onto every word, her heart swelling with the realization that Aspen Cove was not a place but a beacon for people searching for happiness, belonging, and peace. She looked around the room at the kind faces staring back, and a profound sense of contentment filled her.

When Amanda shared her sense of mirrored experiences, Sage let out a hearty laugh that echoed through the cabin, causing Catsby to look up from his slumber by the fire, his feline eyes curious.

"Amanda," Sage said, her laughter dying down, "I wouldn't exactly call our beginnings here similar."

Confused, Amanda tilted her head, inviting Sage to explain further. Sensing Amanda's curiosity, Sage leaned back in her chair, her gaze losing focus as she appeared to journey back to her arrival in Aspen Cove.

"You see," she started, "the day I showed up in Aspen Cove wasn't quite a warm, welcome-to-your-new-life moment. It was more of a black eye and confusion kind of day."

Amanda's eyebrows knitted together at that. "Black eye?" she echoed, her surprise evident.

Sage nodded, a rueful smile curving her lips. "I thought Cannon was hurting his father, Ben. I didn't know the full story and that it was the other way around. Ben was drunk, a mess really, and I ... well, I got in the way."

It took a moment for Amanda to process this. So far, the town seemed such an idyllic place. It was hard for her to imagine such a scene. Yet, Sage's story highlighted the raw, unfiltered truth that not every story was as serene as it appeared on the surface.

"But now," Sage continued, her voice soft but firm, "Ben's sober. He's turned his life around and married Maisey. He's a pillar of the community. All thanks to this town. It has a way of nurturing you, pulling you back from the brink, and guiding you toward the better part of yourself."

Silence settled in the room as Amanda absorbed Sage's words. She looked out the window. It was hard to imagine that real lives with real problems existed behind the pretty facade.

As Sage's words sank in, Amanda was struck by an undeniable sense of respect and awe for the town.

Here was a place that didn't turn a blind eye to its troubled individuals but stepped up to guide them toward a better path. It was not about the picturesque landscape or the charming Christmas decor. It was about the people, their resilience, their capacity to help and heal, that truly made it wonderful—or maybe that was her writer's brain turning something that wasn't idyllic into something that was.

Cannon and Sage took their leave. And while Jackson insisted on shoveling the walkway, she resumed her day, a new sense of inspiration taking root. The stories of Aspen Cove, stories with characters like Cannon, Sage, and Ben, needed to be told. She opened a new document on her laptop. Amanda started to write, her fingers skipping over the keys, ready to bring new stories to life.

Jackson stepped in, snowflakes dusting his hair and shoulders. His cheeks were rosy from the chill, eyes glinting with an intensity that deepened Amanda's appreciation for him. "Got the walkway cleared," he announced, dusting off his jacket. His voice was a soothing echo in the room, harmonizing with the fireplace's whispers.

She closed her laptop. "That's great, Jackson."

His eyes met hers as he nodded. "I have to go, though," he continued, the softness in his tone almost regretful. "Cannon needs help with the other driveways, and Sage wants to get back to the baby."

"Okay. You cooked, and I'll clean up."

He hung his head. "I'm sorry to leave you with the mess."

"It's okay. I don't mind. Besides, I like washing dishes. The act gives my mind a chance to formulate my story."

"Writing again?"

She smiled and nodded. "I'm inspired." Inside, her brain said, *you make an excellent muse.*

"I'm so happy for you." Jackson leaned down and pressed a kiss to her cheek. The coolness of his lips on her warm skin made her heart stutter, and she blinked up at him in surprise.

Pulling back, Jackson's eyes widened as if he hadn't anticipated his action. "I'm sorry, I..." he began, his apology hanging in the air.

"No need to apologize," Amanda responded quickly, her voice teasing despite the butterflies zooming in her stomach. "That might be the best part of my day."

A silent moment passed between them, their shared smile saying more than words ever could. As the moment lingered, Amanda wondered aloud, "Are you going to leave Gunner here with me?"

Jackson shook his head. "I have a shift at the bar tonight, and Gunner is coming along. He loves visiting Mike."

Amanda's eyebrows lifted in confusion. "Who's Mike?"

"Cannon's one-eyed tabby," Jackson clarified, chuckling at her bewildered expression. "Mike minds the bar. Gunner and Mike are good friends."

"Ah, so that's why Gunner's so good with cats," Amanda said, joining him in laughter.

"Yep," Jackson replied. "Well, I better get going. See you later, Amanda."

With that, he stepped back into the winter's chill, the cabin door closing behind him with a soft click. The coziness surrounded Amanda once again, her heart still skipping beats at the memory of his unexpected kiss.

CHAPTER TEN

Jackson navigated the icy bends leading away from the cabin. The truck's heater hummed against the chill of the winter's morning, the familiar vibration beneath his hands a stark contrast to the whirlwind churning in his mind.

The burn in his cheeks had nothing to do with the truck's heater and everything to do with the memory of Amanda's soft cheek against his lips. It was a quick, impulsive action that caught them both off guard. He hadn't planned or thought about it, yet, in retrospect, it was the most natural thing he had done.

Wide-eyed and flushed, he'd left her in the doorway, an echo of his surprise mirrored on her face. His fingers traced the lacing on the steering wheel restlessly, the faint scent of her still clinging to his jacket. He could still feel the ghost of her skin against his, see the sweet surprise in her whiskey-colored eyes, hear the sudden hitch in her breath.

He shook his head, the heavy thud of his heart against his ribs a sharp reminder of his reality. He wasn't supposed to be contemplating the softness of her cheek or the startled beauty of her eyes. He should be focused on the road, on the snowflakes falling from the sky, on anything but Amanda.

"Why did I do that?" he muttered, glancing at Gunner, his faithful shepherd sprawled across the passenger seat. But the dog yawned, his eyes drifting shut once more. He wasn't in any position to offer advice or much-needed wisdom.

Jackson sighed, his gaze shifting back to the road. He flexed his fingers, the steering wheel leather creaking under pressure. Unbidden, Amanda's face floated into his mind: the soft curve of her cheek, the wide-eyed surprise, the perplexed smile that had tugged at her lips after he'd pulled away. And with that image came a pang of longing. "No," he said aloud, forcing the rising emotions back down. This was Amanda, the woman he was supposed to be helping, not complicating her life further.

"Damn," he muttered, a soft chuckle escaping him. What a mess he was getting himself into. He was drawn to her. It was the gentle way she cared, the compassion in her voice when she talked about her writing. The hurt that was there when she spoke about her ex, who, in his mind, was a complete asshole. A soft chuff from the passenger seat drew his attention. "Got any advice, boy?" Jackson asked, casting a quick smile at Gunner. The shepherd perked up, his tail thumping lightly against the door. "Yeah, all you want is a treat from the bakery and bacon from the diner." He reached over and ruffled Gunner's fur. "Not today, boy, but you can snuggle Mike when we get to the bar." As if understanding him, Gunner groaned and covered his head with his paws.

In the silence of the truck, against the backdrop of the peaceful landscape, Jackson found himself on the brink of a situation he hadn't expected to reach. His heart, long buried beneath the hardness of war, was beginning to soften and awaken. And it all traced back to a pair of brown eyes and a soft, surprised gasp.

He shook his head, pushing the swirling thoughts away. Now was not the time. Some neighbors needed his help—the Dawsons, Cade and Abby Mosier, Tilden, and Goldie. Responsibilities awaited, and he couldn't afford to be lost in fantasies about something as unlikely as a lottery win.

As Jackson approached Cannon's house, the truck's wheels crunched over the frozen gravel. The morning sun glinted off the white blanketed lake in the distance. Cannon's silhouette in his dark jacket and jeans contrasted against the backdrop, his broad shoulders hunched over as he tinkered with the snowplow.

Jackson killed the engine, the silence falling like a thick cover over the moment. He stepped out of the truck and squinted at the bright harshness. Gunner followed, his tail wagging as he pranced around.

"Hey, Cannon," Jackson called out, his breath misting in the cold.

Cannon straightened, pulling his gloves off as he flashed a lopsided grin at Jackson. "Took you long enough."

Jackson shrugged. "Had to make sure Amanda was set. Shoveled the walk, in case she needed to get to her car."

Cannon's eyebrows quirked up. "You two seem pretty friendly already. Anything I should know about?"

Jackson hesitated, his gaze falling on Gunner, who was rolling around in the snow. "Nah."

"You look at her like she's cake, and you've been starving for years."

As he helped Cannon realign the plow, he said, "I like her, but not because she's cake, but because she's cool. She's a writer, so her perspective is interesting."

"Be careful when she asks you to pose for her cover. It's a short-run gig. Even Fabio got replaced."

"That's because he got beaked by a goose while riding a roller coaster."

Cannon narrowed his eyes. "How do you know that?"

Jackson laughed. "It broke my mother's heart. Where did you learn about Fabio??"

Cannon's head fell forward. "My mom bought every book that he was on the cover of. I'm sure we still have them in a box somewhere if you need posing inspiration."

"No cover shots for me, but I'd be happy to be her muse." He wasn't sure how much he should share, but he needed a sounding board, so he blurted, "I kissed her goodbye."

The usually stoic man's eyes softened, his brows knitting together. "You kissed her?" He clapped Jackson on the shoulder. "Should I get you a blue ribbon? It was prize-worthy, right?"

"It was a kiss on the cheek." Jackson looked away, focusing on the snow-capped mountains in the distance.

"I take back the ribbon. A peck on the cheek doesn't count. I give those to everyone. Let me know when you kiss her for real. Lips. Tongue. Hands on her hips. Now that's a real kiss."

They climbed inside Cannon's truck, with Gunner taking the space in the middle. As the engine roared to life, they fell into a comfortable silence, the only sounds being the crunch of snow beneath the heavy machinery and Gunner's excited barks. But through it all, Jackson's thoughts were consumed by one thing: kissing Amanda again. This time for real.

They moved from one driveway to the next with friends and neighbors waving their thanks. Abby ran out of the

ONE HUNDRED MERRY MEMORIES

house with a plate of cinnamon rolls and a welcome bag for Amanda. She was the town's beekeeper, creating everything from beauty products to medicinal balms from the honey her bees produced.

At Tilden's and Goldie's, he was forced to say hello to Goldie's fans. She had a vlog, Getting Real with Goldie, showing her life in the mountains. He'd watched a few of her videos and had to admit that she was funny, but it was always entertaining to watch a fish out of water. That made him think about Amanda. She was a city girl who had impulsively moved to the mountains. He wondered if he hadn't come along if she'd still be sleeping in her car, figuring out how to get the raccoon to leave?

"Still thinking about the sort-of kiss?" Cannon's voice broke through his thoughts.

Even though he said, "No," he found himself nodding,

"Take it slow. Sage said she shared some of her stories, and she might be on the rebound, and that never works out well for anyone."

He couldn't argue with that. "I will. I'm Aesop's tortoise."

Cannon looked at him and shook his head. "Who?"

"Never mind." Obviously, Cannon wasn't a reader because if he were, he'd know the reference to mean *The Tortoise and the Hare*. That was one thing he found so appealing about Amanda. She was as familiar with literature as she was with the back of her hand. When he quoted Lao Tsu, he didn't have to teach her about Chinese Taoist philosophers. She knew.

Their last stop was The Big D Ranch, where Sara and Lloyd stood waving from the porch. Lloyd's daughter Lily raced out to say hello, but Lloyd scowled, which sent her running back inside.

"I'm so glad I had a boy," Cannon said. "Little Ben won't ever send me running for my shotgun. If I had a girl, I would tell every boy within a hundred-mile radius to keep their distance."

"You'd teach her to take care of herself, like Viv. No man would ever mess with her." Vivian Armstrong had come to town the same day he had. She scored a job and a husband on a trip to visit her brother Val and his wife, Cameron. In fact, she picked him up on the side of the road. As the head of Vortex Security, she'd hired him to help protect Red Blakely, a band member of a famous pop star living in town.

"Viv is kick ass. I wouldn't want to make her mad," Jackson said.

"Me either."

As the afternoon shadows turned, painting the sky in hues of pink and orange, Cannon headed home, and Jackson picked up his truck and drove to work. He wanted to call Amanda and see how she was faring but didn't have her number. He'd have to remedy that when he got home. Even though he understood their current arrangement was temporary, having a place to return to still brought him a comforting sense of peace.

He parked his truck in front of Bishop's Brewhouse. It was a mainstay of Aspen Cove. Bishop's was the only place to go when the sidewalks rolled up at six. As he opened the door, heat surrounded him. It was a much-welcomed break from the cold outside. Gunner scurried past him in search of Mike. The bar was relatively quiet; a few locals were seated, chatting amongst themselves, their laughter filling the air.

Positioned at the counter, Bowie was hard at work, his large hands deftly pouring a pint for Old Man Larkin, who sat hunched over his usual spot at the end of the bar, his weathered face crinkled in a smile as he exchanged stories with a couple of other regulars.

Seeing Jackson, Bowie lifted his chin in acknowledgment. "Thought you'd gotten lost on the way here."

"Your brother drives like a grandma." He shrugged off his jacket.

"We had some extra driveways to clear, but everyone is good for now."

The familiarity of it all encircled him like a hug. He was in his element with the soft hum of country music playing on the jukebox, the clink of glasses, and the murmur of conversation. Even the sticky bar counter was welcoming. He was new to town, but working in the bar gave him a bird's eye view of the happenings. He'd quickly figured out that if you wanted to stay current, you just had to chill at B's Bakery, Maisey's, or Bishop's Brewhouse. Over the course of his stay, he'd learned enough to qualify as a town historian.

He peeked down at Gunner, who'd found his spot in the corner tucked around Mike. The shepherd was becoming as much a fixture in the bar as the vintage beer signs adorning the walls.

While he got comfortable with the pace of the night, pouring drinks and exchanging pleasantries with the locals, he found himself looking at the clock and hoping it would tick faster. But the night unfolded slowly, the hours marked by the clink of beer bottles and the constant banter of the locals.

Doc Parker walked in and took his regular seat at the end of the bar. His eyes, sharp and bright, focused on a napkin where he'd drawn a grid for tic-tac-toe.

Jackson smiled at the sight. Doc Parker and his beloved game were as much a part of Bishop's Brewhouse as the scarred tables and rickety chairs. In many ways, they represented the heart of Aspen Cove—resilient, enduring, and full of stories that unfolded over rounds of beer and games.

Doc's lips twitched into a grin. "Evening, Jackson!" he said, his voice gruff with age. "Ready to lose?"

Jackson chuckled, his eyes glancing at the tic-tac-toe game. "I wouldn't be so sure, Doc. Might surprise you today."

As he took his place across from Doc, the older man meticulously placed the first O on the grid, a look of complete focus on his face. It was a ritual Doc took seriously, a daily fixture that held a sense of grounding familiarity in the ever-changing tides of life.

The game continued in companionable silence, their moves punctuated by Doc's occasional sip of beer.

Despite his big talk, Jackson lost the game, as he did most nights.

After Doc had celebrated his win with a triumphant wave to the bar and a hearty gulp of his beer, he turned his attention back to Jackson, his eyes taking on a more serious tone.

"Tell me, Jackson, how's Amanda doing?" Doc asked, his voice softer now.

Jackson was taken aback, not expecting Doc to bring up Amanda. Yet, he realized that Doc was like a father to the town.

"She's..." Jackson hesitated, searching for the right words. "She's good." He thought back to the run-in with the critter. "Better now that the squatter's gone." He told the tale to Doc, and by the end, the older man was laughing so hard he was crying.

"And what about you, Jackson? I heard you moved in with her."

The walls of Bishop's Brewhouse had absorbed countless tales over the years, laughter and tears woven into the very fabric of the place. It was more than a bar; it was a sanctuary, a place where the townsfolk thrived, where lives intertwined. It was also a spot where gossip was commonplace. He was sure Cannon had given Doc the lowdown while he was off.

Jackson leaned on the bar, absentmindedly cleaning a glass as Doc set up for another game. He placed his marker and said, "Do you think there's something there?"

He wanted to shake his head, but the idea of doing so seemed like a lie. "It's an exchange of labor for a place to stay. That's all."

Doc chuckled. "In my experience, when two young people get together, they often exchange more." He lifted his brow. "The pharmacy is well stocked."

"I appreciate that, and I will take it slow."

"Ahh." Doc seemed to savor his sip, a satisfied sigh escaping his lips. "Now that's a good beer."

Jackson pointed to the napkin, all gridded and ready. "Are we playing for another?" He couldn't remember a time when Doc paid for a beer, but he always left a nice tip.

"You know, Jackson," he started, setting his glass down. "Sometimes, the best things in life aren't planned. They come when you least expect it. Like a woman with a pink letter. Those letters have changed the lives of many men in this town."

Jackson had a feeling he was about to be counseled. The older man had a knack for offering advice when least expected. And he'd heard about those letters and couldn't deny they were life changers.

"Is there something you want to tell me?"

"Let me share with you a tale about love and relationships. And what better way to illustrate this than through the tic-tac-toe game?"

"Are you trying to win another beer?"

Doc shook his head. "No, son, this isn't about a free beer. It's about something much more important." He picked up the marker and hovered over the napkin. "Love, like tic-tac-toe, is a delicate balance of strategy and timing. Let's imagine the game board as the world of relationships. Each square represents a potential partner or an opportunity to connect." He placed an X in the center square. "Now, the first lesson is about patience. As the first player waits for their turn, taking your time and not rushing into love is crucial. Embrace the beauty of the journey and let connections develop naturally, rather than forcing moves." He handed the pen to Jackson, who placed an O in the top right-hand corner.

Doc pointed to his X and Jackson's O. "Next, we have the importance of balance. The game of love is a give and take." He marked an X to the right of his original and handed Jackson the marker. He knew he'd lose, but they traded turns, with him blocking Doc's easy win. "Love flourishes when everything lines up like the three winning squares in a row. Seek a partner who complements you, both in strengths and weaknesses. Together, you'll form an unbreakable bond, like a winning line in tic-tac-toe." He marked his X and Jackson his O. Clearly, he was losing the game but gaining something far more valuable. "Now, let's talk about resilience," Doc said. "You'll encounter setbacks and losses in love, as you'll encounter losses in tic-tac-toe. But remember, defeat doesn't define you. Learn from each experience, adapt your strategies, and keep playing the game with an open heart." He marked the final X and drew a line connecting them. "Finally, remember that love, like tic-tac-toe, isn't just about winning or losing. It's about the joy of playing, the laughter shared, and the memories made. Embrace the moments, cherish the connections, and find happiness in the process."

Jackson stared at the marked-up napkin and smiled. In the time it took to lose, he'd been schooled in the art of a successful union.

"I'll remember that." He picked up the napkin and tucked it into his pocket.

Doc's eyes met his, a knowing smile playing on his lips. "Something to think about, son."

And with that, Doc stood, his game won, and his beer finished. He nodded at Jackson, placed a five-dollar bill on the bar, and walked away, leaving him with his thoughts and the quiet hum of the bar.

When he closed up for the night, Jackson smiled at the thought of seeing Amanda again. The journey ahead might be uncertain, but he was ready to take it slow, one step at a time. After all, according to Doc, the trip was more important than the win.

As he flicked off the lights, he glanced down at Gunner. "Come on, Gunner. Let's go home."

He drove up the road to the cabin and thought about Doc's words, realizing that while he was right, he was wrong too. Love should never be a game. Playing with someone's heart and mind wasn't ever a good idea. And because Amanda had such a bad experience the last time, he wanted to be upfront and honest about his growing feelings for her. If she didn't share his attraction, nothing was lost or gained. He'd focus on getting her cabin in shape and finding another place to call home.

The lights were still on when he arrived which meant Amanda was awake. He took a deep breath, gathering his courage. He didn't know what the future held or how Amanda would react, but he knew one thing. He had to be honest. For her. For him. For them.

With a final pat to Gunner's head, Jackson walked up the steps and pushed open the front door. It was time to talk.

CHAPTER ELEVEN

Amanda's fingertips flew across the keyboard of her laptop, moving in sync with the cadence of her thoughts. The cabin was wrapped in a peaceful stillness, accompanied only by the gentle crackling of the fire and the tap-tap-tapping of her fingers on the keys. She wove worlds with her words, lost in the embrace of her creative sanctuary when, like a melodic interruption, the low groan of the cabin door pierced the silence.

Her gaze lifted, curiosity lighting her eyes as Jackson strode in like a wayward traveler returning from a distant adventure. Weariness hung on his shoulders like a cloak, tugging at Amanda's heartstrings. A glance at the clock confirmed her suspicions—it was late, almost nearing midnight. Where had the time gone?

As she looked at him, her lips curled into a slight smile. She saw the stubble on his cheeks and chin, which made his chiseled jaw look roguish. The day-old growth gave the impression of a man who didn't have time to waste on shaving but was still effortlessly handsome. His hair was military-short, with just enough length on top to be tousled by the wind. It made him look like he could wield an ax through any fight that stood in his way.

"I didn't expect you to be up," he said.

Amanda closed her laptop. Its presence was now secondary to Jackson's presence. "Well, a writer's mind never slumbers," she replied with a touch of whimsy, her words floating like a playful butterfly. "Besides, inspiration tends to strike at the oddest hours."

A hint of accomplishment crept into Amanda's voice as she directed Jackson's attention to the corner of the room. The bookshelf, once a chaotic assemblage of literary misfits, now stood tall and dignified, like a proud conductor of stories. Once overcrowded and unruly, its shelves now held an organized collection of titles. Amanda had spent hours arranging and rearranging, ensuring each book found its proper place. One shelf remained empty—a welcoming void, waiting to be filled by Jackson's literary treasures.

Jackson's gaze softened, the bookshelf reflected in his eyes like a mirrored promise. His voice, a gentle murmur, carried the weight of gratefulness. "Amanda, this ... it means a lot. Thank you."

"You're welcome."

"I'm glad you're awake because we need to talk."

Amanda's heart skipped a beat, her breath hitching in the stillness. The phrase "we need to talk" reverberated in her mind, evoking memories of past relationships and the stormy clouds they brought. Dread, icy and unyielding, trickled up her spine.

She masked her fear with a reassuring smile, trying to steady her voice. "Is everything alright?" Her words were hesitant and lacked confidence, making her worries linger unsaid.

Jackson hesitated, looking around as if trying to

assemble his thoughts. The silence stretched for seconds that did nothing to quell her anxiety. The atmosphere in their cabin had grown heavy and tense as if all the world's uncertainties were present in that one small space.

"It's about the kiss."

Why did he bring up the kiss?

"Oh." With a flicker of desperation, she sought solace in offering food. Though she tried to maintain composure, her voice quivered as she spoke. "I made my special baked ziti earlier. It's in the fridge. You must be hungry. I'll heat it for you."

She rose, placed two plates on the table, and heated the dish on the stovetop. It was a way to distract herself from the looming unease. Providing nourishment became an unspoken plea for their connection to remain intact, a silent hope that the conversation wouldn't lead to distance or separation.

Underneath her seemingly serene expression, Amanda was a bundle of nerves. She had known Jackson for only three days, yet somehow, he had become an essential part of her life.

"Amanda," Jackson said, his voice heavy with emotion. He reached up and guided her chin toward him until their eyes met. "Stop cooking for now and look at me."

She stared into his eyes—pools of hazel lit by fiery flecks of amber. She didn't see dismissal in them. She didn't see anything but affection.

"You know, when a person says we need to talk, it—"

Jackson growled before he wrapped his hand around the back of her head, and in one swift motion, his lips didn't land on her cheek like earlier but landed on her lips. The kiss was quick and passionate, and her heart stuttered in surprise. His lips were cool from the outside but quickly heated as they moved against hers in a gentle rhythm.

She snaked her arms around his neck as if by instinct and leaned into him with a sigh of contentment. Jackson deepened the kiss, exploring every corner of her mouth. She could feel the tension leaving her body as she allowed herself to enjoy the moment without fear or worry about what he wanted to discuss. At this moment, nothing else mattered except for them.

Jackson broke away with a satisfied smile before pulling back to look into Amanda's eyes again. He leaned forward to place a chaste kiss on her forehead before speaking.

"The hell with talking," he whispered into her ear, sending shivers down her spine. She smiled up at him before burying her face into his chest in embarrassment, and dismissing the idea that Jackson wanted to end their budding relationship over a kiss.

He chuckled lightly before bringing his hands up to stroke her hair, and they stood there, enjoying each other's presence, and allowing all worries to slip away once more.

Amanda leaned back from Jackson's embrace to look up at him, her cheeks flushed. She was rarely at a loss for words, but that kiss had left her speechless.

"I thought you were going to tell me that..." She trailed off, unsure how to finish her sentence.

Jackson smiled down at her. His eyes were alight with emotion. He shook his head before leaning forward and placing another gentle kiss on her forehead.

"No, I wasn't planning to share anything except how much I like you." His voice was full of sincerity. "But I didn't know if you were experiencing the same pull."

She grinned. "And now that we've kissed?"

Jackson's eyes gleamed as he looked down at her, a

gentle smile on his lips. "Now I know you feel it too." He trailed his fingers across her cheek, adding, "You know what they say, show, don't tell."

Being a writer, she lived by those words. "Now what?"

He looked over her shoulder at the baked ziti warming on the stovetop. "We eat," he said with a grin.

Amanda laughed and stepped away from him, feeling light-hearted and truly happy. She scooped out two plates full of ziti and handed one to Jackson before leading him into the living room, where they settled onto the couch together.

As they ate their dinner in comfortable silence, Amanda knew something special was happening between them, something that would last much longer than the evening's meal or tonight's conversation.

After they finished eating, Jackson stood up and returned both plates to the kitchen, where he cleaned them and put them away. He returned to take her hand and walk her to her room. At her door, her heart thudded. Was he expecting more? Did she want more?

He smiled at her and kissed her lips before stepping back. "Goodnight," he said.

She looked up at him, heat rising to her cheeks as she nodded in response before quietly opening the door and slipping inside. He turned away and strode down the hallway, his broad shoulders seeming even wider in the narrow hall.

Amanda closed her door and leaned against it. She breathed deeply, allowing the evening's events to sink in before changing out of her clothes and climbing into bed. She lay there for what seemed like hours, feeling every emotion that had coursed through her during that kiss—fear that it would end all too soon, then excitement when it seemed like it would never end—as if all things were possible at that moment.

Amanda lay in her bed, staring at the ceiling. Despite her exhaustion, sleep seemed like a distant dream. All she could think about was that kiss as she replayed the moment repeatedly.

She removed her blankets and grabbed her phone from the nightstand. She knew exactly who she wanted to talk to—Meg. She quickly punched out a single line of text before hitting send.

I kissed him.

Within seconds, Amanda's phone lit up with a response.

Holy cow! Details!!

Amanda chuckled at her best friend's eagerness. She swiftly tapped her fingers on the keys, moving them across the keyboard.

Amanda's response was filled with playful exaggeration and comedic flair.

Prepare yourself for the epic tale, my dear Meg. It was like a scene out of a romance novel, complete with a swoon-worthy hero, a kitchen transformed by his domestic prowess, and a kiss that made me question if gravity still applied.

A moment later, another text popped up from Meg, causing Amanda to grin.

Oh, honey, I live for these dramatic moments! Go on, spill the juicy details!

Amanda's fingers moved across the screen as she painted a vivid picture of the evening. She described every moment, amplifying everything for Meg's entertainment.

Picture this: Jackson, the culinary knight, transforming the messy kitchen into a shining sanctuary of domestic bliss. And his gaze! Oh, it could rival the intensity of a thousand sunsets. It's like he was trying to solve the mysteries of the universe with just one look. And then, just when I thought my heart couldn't handle any more, his lips brushed against my forehead with a touch that sent tingles down my spine.

Meg's response was swift.

Oh, my, you've stumbled upon the recipe for a swoon-inducing romance! I can practically hear the swooshing of hearts melting around you. Tell me, did you unsheathe his sword?

Amanda read the message twice to make sure she was reading it right. Meg was asking if she'd seen him naked. She chuckled nervously and tiptoed around the truth by responding with:

We've only known each other for three days.

Dots lit up her phone screen, and then Meg replied:

Then you've waited the required time for a Cosmo girl!

Amanda rolled her eyes at Meg's quip but smiled as she pictured Jackson's chiseled features. She bit her lip before continuing.

This is true, but I'm not that kind of girl. I don't kiss on the first date ... or the second!

She waited for what seemed like a lifetime, but it was probably only seconds.

Oh, so you've had several dates?

You caught me.
You know what that makes you?
Amanda laughed out loud.
A ho?
Meg had a different idea in mind because her following text read:
A modern-day princess!
Amanda blushed at the comparison and scrunched up her nose in playful embarrassment. Deep down inside, she knew Meg was right. Her life was an enchanted dream come true.

After Amanda typed good night and hit send, she giggled to herself. Their friendship was a haven of laughter and shared joy.

With a contented sigh, Amanda set her phone aside, turned off the light, and snuggled into her bed. The weight of the day's events caught up with her, pulling her into the comforting embrace of sleep.

CHAPTER TWELVE

Amanda's lips lingered against his, her arms wrapping around his neck, her body pressed so close, they were like one. His eyes snapped open, the rude awakening coming in the form of a cold splash against his forehead. The room was still dim, the first light of dawn creeping in through the window, but the recurring drip, drip, drip echoing around the space was hard to ignore, as was his soaking-wet pillowcase.

"Seriously?" he muttered, squinting up at the discolored patch of wood on his ceiling where last night's snowmelt had found an escape. With a groan of resignation, he tossed off the warm blankets, bracing himself against the sting of the chilly wooden floor beneath his bare feet.

He made his way to his old army footlocker. He knew he had a mason jar full of change and a roll of duct tape. He emptied the coins, trying to keep the clanking to a minimum so he wouldn't wake Amanda, then moved the bed, and placed the jar beneath the leak. The water drip, drip, dripped, creating a sound like a metronome.

"Leaking roofs and chilly mornings, eh, Gunner?" he

murmured to the dog sprawled across his rug. Gunner's tail thumped against the floor in response.

Pulling on his flannel shirt, the cold material prickling his skin, he peered out the unbroken part of his window at the faintly lightening horizon. "Still wouldn't trade this, would we, boy?" Gunner's answering bark echoed in the quiet morning, sealing their pact.

He put his finger to his lips and said, "Shhh, you're going to wake her up." He tugged on his pants and pulled a chair from the corner to right under the leak. He found himself in an absurdly domestic battle—him against the stubborn drip. "If I can get this to slow down, it'll give me time to get into town and gather whatever supplies I need to fix this."

Gunner's head bobbed up and down like he was following Jackson's train of thought.

Standing precariously on an old, squeaky chair with a roll of tape in one hand, he glanced down at Gunner, eyeing the mason jar with sheer fascination.

"You'd think it was a game, huh?" he asked the dog while pressing a strip of duct tape against the leak. Gunner's tongue lolled out in a canine grin. Every escaped drop was met with an eager leap and a snap of Gunner's jaws as if he was on a mission to help catch the falling water before it hit the jar.

His laughter filled the room, bouncing off the walls. "You're a real comedian, you know that?" he told Gunner, bending down to ruffle the dog's wet fur. Believing he'd staunched the flow, he jumped off the chair and landed with a thud. "So much for keeping things quiet."

He tossed the tape on the chair, but it bounced off, hitting the jar and sending a splash of water across the wooden floor.

"Ah, great," he sighed.

Gunner chased the stream, prancing around in delight at the unexpected playtime.

"Of course, you'd find this fun," Jackson said, his frown softening into a smile. He got on his knees, the cold seeping through his jeans as he mopped up the water with a towel. Gunner was beside him in an instant, tail wagging.

He found himself unable to resist the infectious joy of the moment, despite the leaking roof, the damp floor, and his playful dog. He looked around the room, touched by the golden morning light, the memory of Amanda lingering sweetly, and Gunner by his side. This was his life—messy, imperfect, beautiful. The leaky roof was part of the charm.

"And so, the day begins, Gunner," Jackson said, patting his dog's wet head. "Now, how about a short walk before we see Amanda?" Gunner's enthusiastic bark was all the answer he needed. The morning may have started roughly, but there was a whole day filled with possibilities ahead of them.

Gunner shot out when he opened his bedroom door, racing to the front door where he scratched and whined. His need to explore the great outdoors remained constant.

Jackson pulled his jacket from the hook and shrugged it on before opening the door. The morning sun crept over the horizon. Jackson stood at the edge of the porch, his breath fogging up in the brisk morning air. A silver sheen clung to the world, a delicate frost that shimmered under the early sunbeams. Yet, as lovely as the morning was, Jackson couldn't ignore the underlying issue of the day.

He sighed, glancing back at the cabin. With the weather warming, that leak would only get worse. As Jackson looked up, remnants of snow slid off the shingles while icicles melted or fell to the ground.

His dog sat beside him, waiting for permission to leave. Jackson bent down to clip the leash onto Gunner's collar. "Let's get you taken care of first." He'd been assigned Gunner in the army. They'd been partners for years, and when he didn't re-up his enlistment, neither did Gunner. Most dogs had a single handler and weren't good at taking orders from others. He trusted no one on earth more than his dog, but he was hoping to change that.

Their morning walk was a routine. With the brisk air of dawn nipping at their faces, they ventured to the edge of the nearby woods. A faint mist clung to the ground, caught between night and day, and in the distance, he could hear the murmur of a river or possibly runoff from the melting snow.

Gunner was in his element, nosing about in the snow. It was like he was back in the desert, scouting.

"Not a bad way to start the day, huh?" he mused aloud, his voice disappearing into the vast wilderness.

After a few minutes, once Gunner had finished his business, they began their walk back, the leak awaiting him back at the cabin.

Upon returning, he checked the leak and found it had been generous with its gift in his absence. It was no longer a drip but a steady stream, so he grabbed a large pot and pulled out his phone. He needed reinforcements and quick, so he dialed Bowie.

"Do you know what time it is?" Bowie asked.

Jackson laughed. "It's burning daylight time." Their First Sergeant said that when there was work to be done.

"What's the problem?"

He knew Bowie would understand. "Big leak, and it's getting worse by the minute."

"Leave it to you to have a leak in the middle of winter," Bowie laughed.

"I need help with this one." He hated to ask for assistance, but this was a big job, and the faster it got fixed, the dryer he'd stay.

"I'll round the troops. Be there soon."

As Jackson hung up the phone, Amanda appeared from her room wrapped in a soft robe, her hair a mess of curls from sleep. The vision had him holding his breath. He was captivated by her, and all he wanted to do was close the distance and wrap his arms around her, but Cannon's voice echoed in his memory, reminding him to take things slow.

"Did you say leak?" She combed her hand through her hair, brushing it away from her face.

"Yes, the roof is leaking in my bedroom."

She groaned. "I'm sorry. You seem to have gotten the worst deal. First the broken window and now the ceiling." She turned and walked down the hallway toward the kitchen. "I need coffee before I can process."

He rushed past her, pulling out a chair at the table and telling her he'd get a pot started.

"I'm trying to keep my end of the bargain, but when I called the window guy in Copper Creek, he couldn't come out until next week."

"The roof needs more attention than the window right now." He was touched that she was seeing to his comfort and had already scheduled an appointment.

"You're probably right, but duct tape and cardboard won't hold up forever."

"It won't have to. Only until next week." Deciding to shift their focus to something more pleasant, Jackson offered to cook breakfast, to which Amanda responded with an excited cheer. "What girl in her right mind would turn that down, Knight? You're living up to your last name, aren't you?"

"I aim to please." He moved to the refrigerator and took out the fixings for breakfast. Gunner's hopeful eyes followed the bacon. "Not today, buddy."

Amanda drank deeply from her mug and set it down before she rose. "Since we're expecting company and you're already cooking, do you mind if I shower and change before they arrive?"

"Sounds like a plan."

He laid several strips of bacon to sizzle in a pan while he scrambled eggs and toasted bread. By the time she came out looking far better than a woman in sweatpants and a T-shirt should, breakfast was ready.

They enjoyed a peaceful meal with only the slightest interruption when Catsby jumped on the table, and Gunner growled, informing the cat that the area was off-limits. Being a cat, he ignored the dog. Once Catsby realized he wasn't getting any, he jumped down and lay by the fireplace, which reminded Jackson to start a fire.

As if they were on the same wavelength, Amanda said, "How about I do the dishes while you start a fire? I'm sure you'll want a place to warm up."

"Deal," he said. "But it might reach sixty today."

"Seriously? It was like negative one thousand yesterday."

He shrugged. "That's Colorado for you."

The chair legs scraped against the wooden floor when he rose. Within fifteen minutes, the fire was blazing, the kitchen was clean, and a fresh pot of coffee was brewing.

A knock on the door had Gunner darting toward the entrance with an excited bark. The sight of Bowie, Wes Covington, and a few other friendly faces from the town had Gunner's tail wagging in overdrive. Even Katie came with a box of muffins and brownies.

Jackson smiled at Amanda. "The cavalry has arrived."

"And they brought goodies." She invited Katie inside and offered her a cup of coffee.

Everyone said their hellos before Jackson ushered the men out the front door, leaving Amanda and Katie to visit.

They had a truck full of roofing materials, while Bowie brought a ladder and tools. Jackson fell into the supervisor role, with his military background proving useful as he coordinated the repair efforts.

The peaceful tempo of the day was broken only by Gunner's attempts to "help."

After several hours they took a break and enjoyed a muffin and coffee. Katie and Amanda were going through boxes of ornaments. From the conversation, he gathered that they were hitting it off and would probably become fast friends. Katie mentioned her need for a large pine tree for the town square. He followed her gaze out the window to a tree in the middle of the yard.

"One like that would be amazing. It's perfect. I've never seen anything so grand."

Amanda smiled as if she'd planted it herself. "That's why it's staying there. You can take any other tree from my property but not that one. It stood over my first night here like a protective soldier."

Katie smiled. "And now you got a real one."

Amanda nodded. "And he cooks."

Katie's mouth dropped open, and she stared at Bowie. "I may have to trade you in on a newer model." She pointed to Jackson. "That one cooks."

"Oh, I cook, baby, just not in the kitchen."

Katie's pale skin turned beet red.

"Don't you have more work to do?"

They filed out the door to finish the job and leave the women alone.

Throughout the day, his mind drifted back to Amanda, to the vibrant smile that never left her face and the soft laughter that filled the air.

When the work was done, and Bowie and Katie left, he and Wes fixed the sagging porch awning. Wes, the last to leave, gave Jackson a friendly pat on the shoulder. "Take care of that pretty lady, Knight." He winked, a knowing smile on his face. Jackson laughed at the well-meaning comment, acknowledging the truth it held.

"I'm trying to." He didn't have a lot of money. He had little to offer anyone except his honesty, time, and love. He hoped that would be enough.

As the door closed behind him, the cabin seemed to take a deep breath, settling into the quiet that had become a rare commodity throughout the day. Gunner had already claimed his spot by the fireplace with Catsby in the chair above him.

Amanda was in the kitchen, her hands busy washing dishes. Seeing her standing there, lost in thought, brought forth a rush of emotions that Jackson had been trying to ignore all day.

"How about some hot chocolate?" he asked.

She smiled and nodded. "I'm happy to get it for you."

He shook his head. "Not for me, for you."

He filled a mug with milk and heated it in the microwave. When it came out steaming, he added cocoa, sweetener, and a dash of salt and whisked it until it was blended.

"See if you like this. It's my mom's recipe," he said, his eyes meeting hers. The grateful smile she gave him made his heart flutter. Offering to finish the dishes, he shooed her toward the couch. "Go enjoy the fire with Gunner. I'll be there in a minute."

"But you worked outside all day."

He nodded toward the living room. "Go. I'm fine."

A few minutes later, Jackson joined her, while Gunner curled beside her, resting his head on her lap as she absentmindedly stroked his fur. The sight of their companionship brought an unfamiliar squeeze to his heart. Gunner was like his kid, and he could never be with anyone who didn't love his kid as much as he did. Looking at the two together told him that wasn't something he needed to worry about.

"Can you believe that Katie has Bea's daughter's heart and Bowie was once engaged to the heart's original owner, Brandy? I'm a writer and can't make up anything that good."

He nodded. "I know. Wild, right? I met Bowie just after he entered the army. Shortly after he lost Brandy. It was a battle for him, but he came out on the other side."

"It's super swoony."

"Swoony?"

"Romantic." She looked at him with big brown eyes and said, "I want a fairytale ending someday."

Same here. And for the first time in a while, he longed for that potential future. It was a future that hadn't crossed his mind until Amanda entered his life—a future brimming with love, camaraderie, and a profound feeling of belonging. He realized he was prepared to champion her, him, and their bond.

CHAPTER THIRTEEN

Days later, Amanda sat in her favorite armchair and cradled a steaming mug of hot chocolate. Its rich scent wafted toward her, mingling with the pervasive scent of aged pine and wood smoke. She blew across the surface, dispersing the tiny marshmallows bobbing like little sugary lifeboats before taking a careful sip.

The bittersweet concoction melted on her tongue, warming her from the inside out. She allowed her gaze to travel across the room, her writer's mind already painting a vivid picture of the coming Christmas season.

Her eyes lit as she envisioned the cabin transformed into a veritable Christmas wonderland. Strands of twinkling lights, each bulb a little droplet of radiance, would be strung along the rustic wood-beamed ceiling and around the windows, a reverie of color reflected on the glass panes, cascading a soft glow onto the snow outside.

She imagined delicate snowflakes crafted from paper and glitter suspended from the ceiling. They'd sway in the rising heat from the fireplace, creating a mesmerizing, almost hypnotic, spectacle of light and movement.

A robust Christmas tree would stand against the far wall where the fireplace was situated. Its branches, green and thriving, would cradle various ornaments, combining Bea's vintage treasures and her additions. Each ornament would tell a story—a nostalgic echo of the past meeting the present. She could almost hear the whispers of laughter, shared tales, and carols lacing the air.

A contented sigh escaped her as she took in the cabin—her cabin. The quiet creaking of the old wood settling, the crackle of a log in the fireplace, and the rustling of the pine trees outside the window as they swayed in the gentle wind seemed to hint at the cabin's hidden potential.

"But oh, Catsby," she said to the feline curled up on the rug nearby, "It's going to be a lot of work. But I think ... I think it'll be worth it. You'll have so much fun with everything I put on the tree." She thought about their first Christmas together when he climbed up the center of the tree, causing it to become unstable. It crashed to the ground, scattering the ornaments. Finding them was Catsby's greatest adventure that year. He was still finding bits and pieces into February.

The canvas of the cabin was bare, and her vision was clear. Christmas awaited.

The gentle buzz of her phone drew Amanda out of her festive reverie. A bright smile spread across her face at the sight of Meg's name on the screen.

She swiped to answer, the warm familiarity of Meg's voice instantly causing the room to feel vibrant and alive.

"Hey girl, what's shakin'," Meg said with a chuckle that reverberated through the phone.

"Oh, the connection is good today." It was touch and go in the mountains. "I'm living the dream. Just sitting here drinking hot cocoa and figuring out how I want to decorate the tree for Christmas."

The ensuing conversation was a warm blend of laughter and friendly teasing. She shared her plans for decorating the cabin for Christmas, her voice animated with excitement.

Eventually, the conversation swerved to an inevitable topic—Jackson. "So, tell me. Have you done it yet?" Meg asked, her voice echoing with a smirk Amanda could almost visualize.

A shiver that had nothing to do with the weather ran up Amanda's spine. A rush of heat flooded her cheeks, an unexpected reaction that had her flustered. She ran a hand through her hair, her gaze drifting toward the window and the view beyond where she knew Jackson was busy with his work.

"Well," she began, a coy smile playing on her lips, "Let's just say that the fireplace isn't the only thing creating sparks around here." She could feel Catsby's eyes on her, his feline curiosity piqued by her sudden coyness.

Meg's laughter was like the jingle of Christmas bells, tingling through the phone and filling the cabin with its contagious cheer. "And you thought your girlie bits had left with Daniel."

"Oh, I knew they were still here, but they haven't come out to play in a long time." She cleared her throat. "They are still hiding but are interested in making a debut one of these days."

"But you live together. Surely there's been some 'show me yours, and I'll show you mine.'"

She laughed. "Nope, we are taking it slow."

"There's slow, and then there's sloth. Get a move on it before the cobwebs take over."

Amanda laughed. "It will all happen when the time is right. We're just getting to know each other and enjoying that process. I think people rush to the finish when all the good stuff happens in the middle."

Meg groaned. "But the finish feels so damn good."

"I do like a good finish."

"And where might he be at this time?"

Amanda's heart warmed at the thought of Jackson. She looked out the window toward the forest where he'd gone. The midday sun peeked through the evergreens, casting dappled light patterns on the ground. Her mind's eye pictured him there, sturdy in his flannel and boots, his breath clouding around him in the cold winter air as he inspected each tree with a practiced eye.

"He's out finding the perfect Christmas tree for the town square," Amanda answered, her voice carrying a note of pleasure she hadn't expected. Her heart was strangely full, thoughts of Jackson interwoven with the spirit of community and tradition. The magic of it all settled deep within her bones.

"You're donating a tree to the town?"

"It's the least I could do. They came here and replaced my roof and fixed my porch, and no one would let me pay them. A tree from the surrounding forest seems a small price for their generosity."

A sense of wonder filled Amanda. She had seen cities with skyscrapers touching the clouds and had been in places where the lights never dimmed, and the noise never ceased. Yet, here she was, in a small town tucked away in the mountains, mesmerized by thoughts of a man chopping down a tree.

She glanced around the room at the rustic wooden beams and the stone fireplace. The cabin itself was a witness to the town's history, a piece of heritage entrusted to her by Bea. Her fingers grazed the worn wooden table, the grain rough under her touch. Each nick and stain told a story, whispers of times and people past.

Her mind formed an image of a tall evergreen adorned with multicolored lights and ornaments, standing proudly in the town square while the townsfolk sang carols around it. Pine, mixed with hot cider and gingerbread, filled her senses. She could almost hear the town's joyous laughter, their voices raised in melodious song, and at the center of it all would be Jackson's tree—her tree.

Lost in her thoughts, she didn't realize Meg was talking until she heard her name. "...da, Amanda, you there?"

"Yes, sorry, Meg, got lost in thought," she confessed, a sheepish smile on her lips. "I was just imagining the tree lighting ceremony and how wonderful it will be."

Her voice trailed off, her gaze drifting back to the window. Somewhere out there, among the towering evergreens, Jackson was fulfilling a tradition, becoming a part of the town's living history. And she was slowly integrating into it too. The thought warmed her more than any mug of hot chocolate ever could.

"And you, my dear, will be in the middle. Embrace it. It's going to be wonderful," Meg said. "Then come home and write about it."

"I've written so much in the last few days. It's unbelievable how this place inspires me."

"Doesn't hurt that you have the brawny man giving you kisses and cooking you breakfast."

No, that didn't hurt, but it was more than Jackson. It was as if the air around her infused her with the creativity she'd been missing.

A truck appeared, and she knew Jackson's window had

arrived. "I've got to go. The window repair guy is here. Love you."

"Love you more," Meg responded.

The click of the call ending resonated in the quiet cabin, punctuating the shift in Amanda's thoughts. She opened the door to let the repair man in and showed him to Jackson's room.

She loved how tidy Jackson was and figured that came from his years in the military. His bed was made, and nothing was out of place. She lifted her nose in the air and inhaled. The room smelled like him. He was a mixture of musk and pine and romance.

Leaving the man to do his job, she returned to the living room. A smile played on her lips as she looked around, her eyes taking in everything she'd placed on the shelves, from her beloved typewriters to her treasured books. Even Jackson's shelf was filled with Louis L'Amour, James Patterson, and a few Poes and Hemingways sprinkled in.

With a sense of purpose, she padded across the room to the closed doors she had yet to explore. These were Bea's old storage closets, yet to be explored since she'd moved in. Catsby, ever her silent companion, followed her to the closet, his tail curled up high in a question mark.

She turned the doorknob, the metal cool under her palm, and pulled open the door. The scent of time, tinged with cedar and dust, floated out. In front of her were shelves filled with cardboard boxes and covered items, the past tucked away, waiting to be rediscovered. The closet was a time capsule holding relics of Bea's life, and Amanda felt a sense of reverence wash over her. She was about to uncover pieces of a woman she'd never met who had changed her life in unimaginable ways.

The first box she opened was filled with more

Christmas ornaments. Amanda lifted them, revealing painted glass balls, wooden figures carved with meticulous detail, and strings of twinkle lights. Each piece was a snapshot of a holiday season past, the joy and happiness of the festivities held within. As she lifted each ornament to the light, her heart fluttered.

Beneath the box of ornaments, she found a stack of family photographs. She perused them, each image showing Bea's life. There were pictures of a younger Bea, her face radiant with joy and her eyes brimming with life. Others showed Bea with friends, their faces alight with laughter. There were images of the town. Amanda had to admit that it hadn't changed much.

"Look, Catsby," Amanda said, holding up a picture of Bea with a tabby cat that looked eerily similar to Catsby. The cat looked up from his spot on the floor, his green eyes seemingly understanding the significance of the picture. "I bet you would have loved Bea."

As Amanda delved into the memories left behind by another woman, she felt a deep connection with Bea, a profound sense of kinship. Bea had once been an integral part of this town, just as Amanda hoped to be. The realization moved through her, bringing tears to her eyes as she grasped the immense significance of it all.

Her fingers brushed against a set of recipe cards. She ran her fingers over the handwritten menus, feeling the indentations of the pen on the paper, almost as if Bea herself had just written them.

In her mind, she saw Bea standing in a kitchen that smelled like cinnamon and vanilla, a wooden spoon in her hand as she mixed the ingredients for her famous sugar cookies. The cookies would be shaped like Christmas trees and snowflakes, with a generous dusting of colored sugar.

The imagined taste of them on her tongue was so vivid it made her drool.

"This one," she began, pulling out a recipe card for a Christmas ham. The smell of roasting meat and the tangy sweetness of pineapple glaze filled her senses. "This must have been Bea's special Christmas dinner recipe. I bet the whole house filled with its spicy notes, and everyone would be waiting impatiently to dig in."

She continued in this fashion, every object she picked up adding a new story to her narrative. An old photograph showed a younger Bea in a winter coat, laughing as she held a gigantic snowball above her head. Amanda mused aloud about the fun snowball fight that must have occurred that day. She imagined Bea, breathless with laughter, the chill of the snowball in her hands, the taste of snowflakes on her tongue.

Through her narration, Bea's spirit seemed to fill the cabin, her laughter ringing in the silence, her joy reflected in the twinkling of the Christmas ornaments, and her love in the handwritten recipes.

Amanda lost track of time as she continued to sift through Bea's treasures. Her mind became a playground of fictional stories, piecing together fragments of Bea's life, her joys, and her Christmases. She took in the ornaments, a silent witness to the passage of time and the legacies left behind.

Just as she was about to delve into the next box, her phone buzzed, jolting her out of her reverie. The shrill tone cut through the air, capturing her attention. Glancing at the screen, she saw Katie's name flashing, and excitement coursed through her.

"Hi, Katie," she answered, trying to sound casual, even though she was excited to hear from her new friend.

"Amanda, I hope I'm not disturbing you?" Katie's voice was as warm as Amanda had expected.

"Not at all," she reassured, her gaze wandering back to Bea's belongings. "I was just going through some of Bea's old things."

"Oh, that sounds like a treasure hunt," Katie said. "I'm calling to invite you over to the diner tomorrow. We're planning the town's Thanksgiving celebration, and we could use your help."

Amanda hesitated. As much as she already loved Aspen Cove and its friendly residents, she was a newcomer and couldn't shake the feeling of being an intruder, someone who had yet to grasp the traditions and customs.

"You are as much a part of this town as any of us now," Katie said as if hearing Amanda's thoughts. "We'd be thrilled to have your input," she assured her, leaving no room for doubt. "Honey, in a town as small as ours, everyone's a newcomer at some point. This is your home too."

Those words, so simple yet full of meaning, hit Amanda like a gust of wind. Her home. This was her home now. And these people, they were her neighbors, her friends.

"Thank you, Katie," she murmured, her voice choked with emotion. "I'd love to help."

"Great!" Katie's cheerfulness was infectious. "We'll see you tomorrow then."

Just as the call ended, the window repairman finished. She paid his bill and locked the door behind him.

The room was quiet now, save for the crackling fire and Catsby's gentle purrs.

Amanda's gaze fell on her laptop, left open on the small writing desk she'd placed by the window. A blank page awaited her in the word processing software, its emptiness mirroring the new chapter of her life yet to be written. She was now more than ready to fill those pages, to add her own experiences and her own stories to the rich history of the cabin.

Sitting at the desk, she took one last look around the place. Her eyes lingered on Bea's trinkets. Her mind filled with their imagined tales. Her gaze then moved to Catsby, still sleeping soundly. With a renewed sense of purpose, she placed her hands on the keyboard, ready to expose the essence of the town's story.

She began to type, her fingers tapping across the keys as the first words of her new chapter took shape.

CHAPTER FOURTEEN

The smell of sizzling bacon and coffee nudged Jackson from his sleep. Blinking awake, he lay in bed, the morning sun casting a warm, golden glow through the new window. He listened to the unfamiliar but pleasant sounds in the kitchen —the clinking of dishes, the hiss of eggs frying in a pan, and the quiet hum of a contented woman—Amanda.

Gunner stirred from his spot at the foot of the bed, his tail thumping against the wooden frame. With a soft whine, the dog hopped off the bed and padded toward the door, clearly drawn to what was happening in the kitchen.

Pushing the quilt aside, Jackson followed Gunner, barefoot and shirtless. His dark hair was tousled from sleep, but his hazel eyes were alert, taking in the sight of Amanda bustling around the kitchen. She hummed to herself, the melody blending with the cooking sounds.

"Good morning," he said, his voice still rough from sleep. He smiled as she jumped, then turned to face him with a wide grin. Ever the opportunist, Gunner nudged his snout against Amanda's hand, wagging his tail in hopes of a scrap of bacon.

"Morning, sleepyhead," Amanda replied, giving Gunner a quick scratch behind the ears before returning her attention to the stove. She gestured toward the counter with the spatula in her hand. "Hope you're hungry."

That was how their day began, sharing a breakfast of scrambled eggs, crispy bacon, and thick slices of toast. She moved around the kitchen, chatting and laughing as if she had been doing it for years. Gunner settled at their feet, his eyes never straying from the bacon on the table.

As they finished their breakfast, Jackson leaned back in his chair, studying Amanda over the rim of his coffee mug. "Thanks for taking care of the window repair," he said.

She shrugged, her cheeks turning a delicate pink. "It was no trouble. The least I could do was offer you a warm place to sleep after you've been working hard on all the outdoor repairs."

"I had a lot of help with that." He smiled. "I hope I didn't wake you when I came in from the bar last night."

"No, you didn't," she reassured him, her eyes warm. "I wrote until nearly midnight and then crashed. I'm a pretty sound sleeper."

"Good to know," he said, his gaze lingering on her before he leaned back in his chair, his body relaxed from the breakfast she had cooked. A comfortable silence settled between them as they finished their coffees, the pleasant morning taking a slow, unhurried pace.

"Now that the outdoor work is mostly done until spring, it's time to focus on the inside," he said, mentally compiling a list of necessary repairs that awaited them. He had already noticed the worn-out hardwood floors that shifted under their steps. Some floorboards needed to be replaced entirely, while others might be salvageable with sanding and refinishing.

He considered the old fireplace, too, with its soot-stained stones and askew mantle. It would need a thorough cleaning and possibly some mortar work to ensure safety and efficiency.

The kitchen, despite its retro appeal, was in desperate need of modern touches.

And then there were countless smaller tasks—tightening a loose doorknob, fixing a leaky faucet, replacing flickering light bulbs. No matter how small, each job was a step toward making the cabin more comfortable and livable.

"I know there's a lot to do, but..." Amanda's eyes shimmered in the golden sunlight, and a shimmer of eagerness flickered within their depths. "Would you mind cutting down a tree for us?" she asked, her voice barely more than a whisper. "For Christmas, I mean."

Surprise washed over him, quickly replaced by warm affection. A Christmas tree. He hadn't given it much thought, but the cabin would be incomplete without it. A smile broke across his face, and he nodded, already picturing the festive decoration filling their living room with holiday cheer.

THE MORNING FOUND them trudging through the snow-covered forest, with each breath coming out in little clouds. Jackson led the way, with Gunner bounding around them, his exuberance adding to the joy of their quest.

During their search, a real spark of playfulness ignited between them. Jackson noticed Amanda bending down, her gloved hands forming a handful of snow into a perfect sphere. A glint of mischief lit her eyes, reflecting off the glittering snowflakes adorning her dark hair.

"Hey, Jackson," she called out, a grin curling at the corners of her mouth. "Catch!" With that, she launched the snowball in his direction. It landed on his chest, scattering powdery snow over his flannel shirt.

He stared in mock surprise, then looked up to see her laughing, the sound flowing like the nearby mountain stream. It was infectious, and he found himself chuckling along with her. He shook his head, a broad grin on his face. "So that's how it's going to be, huh?"

Before she could respond, Jackson stooped down to gather his arsenal. Amanda squealed and turned to run, but not before he landed a well-aimed snowball on her back.

Their laughter echoed through the forest, replacing the usual silence with joy. They darted amongst the snow-dusted trees as snowballs whizzed through the space between them.

"Dodge this!" Amanda challenged, narrowly missing him as he ducked behind a tree.

"Nice aim, but you'll have to do better than that!" Jackson said, returning fire.

Now and then, Jackson would glimpse Amanda's flushed cheeks, her smile brighter than any Christmas light, and his heart would skip a beat. This unexpected snowball fight, this shared moment of childlike fun, was weaving a layer of happiness into their day he hadn't anticipated.

It was a simple, unadulterated joy, and to Jackson, it was like a precious gift, one he was more than ready to unwrap.

The snowball fight ended as abruptly as it began, their laughter fading into the fresh snow crunching under their boots. Their breaths, previously fogging up in the sharp bouts of laughter, now emerged in slow, steady puffs, filling the silent air around them. As they ventured deeper into the forest, a soft rustling sound pierced the silence, causing them both to freeze.

Jackson reached out, his fingers curling around Amanda's arm. He pulled her behind a large pine tree with a gentle tug, pressing his body against hers as they huddled behind the bark.

"Shhh," he whispered, lifting a finger to his lips, his eyes twinkling with a playful hint of adventure. Amanda's heartbeat thrummed against her ribcage, a silent sonata echoing close to Jackson.

Jackson silently pointed toward a break in the trees with his other hand. There, in the frosted foliage, stood a curious deer. It stared in their direction, its large, innocent eyes reflecting the muted winter sun. It was a remarkable creature, with its russet brown coat contrasting the stark white of the winter forest around them.

Neither dared to breathe, the sight of the gentle creature holding them in rapt attention. The world seemed to pause around them, the moment's magic suspending them in a shared bubble of wonder.

"Wow," Amanda breathed out in a whisper. Her eyes were wide with awe, the corners crinkling in pure delight.

Jackson nodded in agreement, his gaze alternating between the breathtaking view of the deer and the woman beside him, who seemed to have brought the magic with her into his life.

But as quickly as the moment began, it ended. The deer, perhaps catching their scent or sensing their presence, gave one last lingering look before darting off into the underbrush, its tail flashing white before disappearing completely.

They remained still for a moment longer, the echo of the encounter reverberating between them. Jackson thought these unexpected moments, these shared experiences, were slowly braiding their lives together, one enchanted thread at a time.

Shaking off their surprise, they resumed their search for the perfect Christmas tree. With Jackson's knowledge of the forest, it didn't take long for them to find the right one. A tall, robust pine tree stood before them, its branches lush and green, covered in a light dusting of snow.

With a nod of approval, Jackson set to work. He felled the tree and trimmed it to the perfect size, ensuring it would fit comfortably in their living room. Once they returned it to the cabin, he constructed a sturdy base, so it would stay upright and stable throughout the holiday season.

Next, they set out to decorate their tree. Laughter echoed through the cabin, punctuated by Amanda's animated storytelling. Nothing was ever more perfect.

Amanda unwrapped each ornament from its box, holding them with the delicacy of a curator handling precious artifacts. Her eyes gleamed with an energy that breathed life into the room. As she lifted each piece, she spun a web of possible tales it could tell.

One vibrant red cardinal ornament held a story of a childhood pet that loved to sing in the early mornings. A glass angel brought a tale of an elderly grandmother who had passed down wisdom and love. A worn-out, painted wooden sleigh told a tale of adventures in the deep, snowy woods.

Jackson listened, captivated, as she brought each inanimate object to life with her words, each narration creating a vibrant palette of Christmas possibilities.

As she tried to reach a high branch, he laughed. In a smooth motion, he took the ornament from her hand. Their fingers brushed against each other, electricity passing between them. Jackson blinked, covering his surprise by quickly placing the decoration on the tree.

The tree came alive under Amanda's imaginative influence, highlighted by the soft, muted light that spilled through the cabin windows. The melting snow outside made rivulets of water down the glass, lending magic to the atmosphere within.

"There's a meeting regarding the Thanksgiving dinner in town, and I hope they let me make Bea's special holiday ham." Amanda looked sadly at the clock and sighed. "I have to go, or I'll be late."

The sudden break caught Jackson off guard. He stood, brushed off imaginary lint from his jeans, and cleared his throat. "Would you like to grab a beer at Bishop's Brewhouse afterward?" He tried to keep his tone casual but felt like a teenager asking the prettiest girl in high school out for a date.

A warm smile spread across her face. "I'd love to."

Jackson's heart pounded as she grabbed her coat. It wasn't the beer he was looking forward to. It was the promise of sharing more laughter, stories, and stolen moments under the neon lights.

As Amanda left the cabin, he stood by the window, the traces of her presence fading. A glance at the decorated tree brought a smile to his face. The day had started with a simple meal and had ended with shared memories woven around a Christmas tree. He looked forward to what the night might bring.

AS THE EVENING FELL, Jackson was behind the bar, pouring drinks and sharing casual conversation with the locals. The bar was vibrant with laughter, underscored by the warm hum of music playing in the background. Friends of Dalton were playing pool. Though they looked like the Sons of Anarchy, they were nice guys.

Just as he was about to text Amanda to see when she was coming, the bar door swung open, and in walked Samantha, a renowned singer known as Indigo. As she made her way toward the stage, whispers followed in her wake, and the conversations around the room hushed to murmurs. Samantha had a way of making every night she performed feel special.

Right on cue, Amanda walked inside the bar. She took in the scene, her eyes widening when she noticed Samantha setting up on the stage with the band. She walked up to the bar, nudging his arm. "Is that ... is that really Indigo?" she asked, pointing discreetly toward the stage.

He grinned, amused by her excitement. "The one and only. Her real name is Samantha, and she comes occasionally on karaoke nights with the band. She married a local named Dalton. She spent some of her childhood here."

Without missing a beat, Amanda said, "You think she'd mind if I said hello?" The words rushed out in her excitement.

He shook his head. "Not at all. Come on. I'll introduce you."

Leading Amanda to the stage, he introduced her to Samantha, who greeted her with a warm smile and a hug. Amanda eagerly engaged the singer in conversation, her writer's mind visibly churning as Samantha shared about how she'd returned to town to find herself.

Amanda hung onto every word as Samantha told her how she'd walked off the stage during a concert, got into a car, and drove to Aspen Cove because it was the one place she'd felt happy as a child.

Back behind the bar, Jackson kept a watchful eye on Amanda. Her animated gestures, her soak in the moment demeanor—she was in her element. He imagined the type of story she was creating from this encounter, or the characters she might be conjuring up from the colorful personalities in Bishop's Brewhouse.

When she left, he walked her to the door and kissed her like his life depended on it. Maybe it was because she brought so much life into his. When he walked back into the bar, everyone still there clapped and hooted, making him feel both embarrassed and lucky to have a woman that could cause such a stir.

When the bar's doors closed, and the last patrons had trickled out, Jackson stood outside the bar with the cold burning his exposed skin. He locked the door behind him, the metallic click echoing in the quiet street. The night was clear, the stars glittering above like distant diamonds against the black velvet canvas of the sky.

The journey back to the cabin was quiet, filled with almost palpable energy. He kept his eyes focused on the road, but his mind was filled with thoughts of Amanda.

He arrived at the cabin, a welcoming silhouette against the melting blanket of snow. He found her at the door waiting for his arrival. He parked, and he and Gunner walked to the house.

"I waited to thank you," she said from the doorway. Her smile was like a lighthouse beam. "That was a perfect night."

He knew the night could be exceptional but was still trying to take it slow.

"I'm glad you had fun. If you're closing things up, I'll

walk you to your room." He wrapped his arm around her shoulders and led her down the hallway. As they stood at her bedroom door, Jackson leaned in, his gaze lingering on her lips. He tilted her face to meet his, and their mouths met in a sweet, lingering kiss.

It was a simple kiss, nothing more than a press of lips, yet it carried a promise, a silent confession of things unsaid. It wasn't their first kiss, but it was a turning point, a gentle crossing of a line that signaled a deeper connection and more to come.

Amanda seemed to feel it too. When they pulled apart, her breath hitched, her eyes wide and vulnerable as they met his. There was a hunger there, a longing that matched his own. The last of his self-restraint shattered when she bit her lip, and her gaze dropped to his. He placed one last gentle kiss on her cheek, whispering a husky goodnight before he turned away.

CHAPTER FIFTEEN

Amanda had always revered the quiet solace of early mornings, the muted whispers of a world still wrapped in slumber. This time was a haven for her, a peaceful sanctuary where she was entangled in the delicate trappings of her imagination. It was a time when her thoughts, unbound by the distractions of the waking world, ebbed, and flowed freely, painting a vibrant mosaic of words and tales in her mind.

She found her usual spot at the small desk by the window. Outside, nature was gradually awakening, a choreographed ballet of life that took place every dawn. Birds started serenading the approaching day; their songs wove through the morning air, intertwining with the soft rustling of leaves as if exchanging sleepy tales of the previous night's adventures.

She settled in, her laptop open in front of her, its screen bathed in the glow of the dawning day. Her fingers hovered over the keyboard. And then they began their dance, a graceful waltz of letters and spaces, giving life to the echoes in her mind.

Her characters, still sleepy-eyed and rumpled from the confines of her imagination, began to stir, and take shape under her gentle guidance. They emerged from the shadowy corners, stretching and yawning, whispering their stories into her ear. Their lives, dreams, sorrows, and triumphs were all spun into existence in the muted colors of the early morning.

As Amanda delved deeper into her story, a movement at her feet pulled her from her literary world. Catsby had claimed his spot on the chair next to the corner, his half-closed eyes filled with curiosity. A soft, rumbling purr vibrated from him, a pattern syncing with Amanda's fingers tapping on the keys.

Catsby's tail curled around his body, and his gaze locked onto Amanda. It was as if the feline was conveying a silent message—his look seemed to say, *Proceed; I'll just be here, quietly ruling my kingdom.*

Basking in the harmony of bird songs, the gentle rustle of the world outside, and the steady purring of Catsby, Amanda smiled. She looked at the words flowing across her screen, at Catsby's contentedly curled form, then out the window where the dawn was slowly unfurling its radiant colors. And she knew, without a doubt, that this moment, this experience, this book was perfect.

She put her mug down and watched Jackson through the window as he moved in the half-light of morning. He was stacking wood, his actions precise and practiced. Seeing him work stirred something in her chest—admiration for his dedication and determination. But it was time to focus on her laptop, why she'd come to Aspen Cove in the first place—to write a story. The peaceful morning made it easy for her creativity to flow. Heck, she wrote at all hours of the day and night here. If sleep weren't a necessity, she'd write around the clock.

When she rechecked the time, hours had passed, and it was nearing lunchtime. She needed to go into Copper Creek and get supplies for Thanksgiving. A list of items came to mind—sweet potatoes, marshmallows, cranberries, ham...

She was mulling over her shopping list when Jackson's voice drifted to her from the door. "Hey," he said in a rich timbre that tugged her from her thoughts. He appeared in the doorway, muscles pronounced under his worn flannel shirt, his eyes filled with a muted curiosity as they glanced at her screen. "Hope I'm not interrupting your creative process."

A soft chuckle slipped past her lips. "Not at all, Jackson," she reassured him, closing her laptop and welcoming the break. Her eyes met his, their whiskey depths reflecting the growing light outside. "I was just thinking about heading out soon. I need to get supplies for Thanksgiving—stuff The Corner Store won't carry."

His eyebrows lifted. A thoughtful frown etched on his handsome face as he leaned against the door frame. "Heading to Copper Creek?" he asked, the faintest hint of hope lacing his words. At her nod, he let out a soft breath, a nearly inaudible sigh. The silence hung briefly before he offered, "I can drive you there. I have a few errands to run myself."

Her heart thumped against her ribs, and her chest filled with a giddy swirl of excitement. "That would be great." Recovering her composure, she asked, "Will your errands take you anywhere exciting?"

He smiled. "I need to stop by the bookstore here in town to get something I ordered." His voice was casual, as if picking up a book was as mundane as fetching a gallon of milk.

"Bookstores are my kryptonite," she confessed, her lips stretching into a broad grin. She couldn't deny the thrill coursing through her veins at the thought of browsing through rows and rows of books, getting lost in their worlds.

He laughed, a rich sound that filled the cabin. "Then I guess it's settled," he said, his voice softer now. "Leave in fifteen?"

Nodding, she retreated to her room, her mind racing. She found herself in front of her closet, eyes scanning the neatly hung clothes. It wasn't a date, she reminded herself. But as her fingers trailed over her selection, lingering on a comfortable flannel shirt, her heart thrummed a different tune. She pushed aside the thrill bubbling within her. This was just a casual outing with Jackson, nothing more.

But as she pulled on her boots, securing the laces with a final tug, she held onto the spark of hope kindling in her heart. It wasn't a date, but that didn't mean it couldn't be something just as special.

The short journey to the bookstore was filled with light-hearted chatter, creating a warm atmosphere. As they stepped inside the establishment called B's Books, a bell jingled overhead, announcing their arrival.

Like the breath of a thousand stories, the smell of aged paper and ink wrapped around Amanda, placing her in a comforting embrace of nostalgia. The bookstore was a treasure trove of forgotten tales and unexplored worlds, the spines of countless books lining the wooden shelves that reached to the ceiling.

As she delved deeper into the store, her eyes were drawn to a splash of pink nestled within a polished wooden frame hanging on a nearby wall. The light streaming through the nearby window caught the glass covering, casting a soft glow on the handwritten letter displayed beneath. She recognized the stationary, a familiar pale pink. Amanda found herself reading the words penned by a hand that spilled love and sorrow in equal measures.

Dear Recipient,

I know it's unusual for a donor's family to reach out to the beneficiary, but I wanted you to know a little about your gift giver.

They kept the registry private, and if this letter found you, it means I hired the right person for the job. A good PI is like a good bra. It's working behind the scenes, but it's holding up its end of the bargain. To track you down could be considered intrusive, but on some level, you became family the moment the gift was received.

I thought I'd let you know a little about Brandy. She was warm sunshine on a cold winter's day, a flicker of light in a dark moment, and as sweet as Abby's honey.

She was adopted, but somehow, I knew she was born to be mine. Brandy lived fully, loved deeply, and laughed heartily. While she was taken far too soon, knowing she lives in others makes the loss bearable.

My hope is that her sweetness flows through you. Smile more than you frown, laugh more than you cry, and give more than you take. Most importantly, have a long and fruitful life.

With love,

Bea

When she finished reading, a slow sigh slipped past her lips. The earnestness in the words pulled at her heartstrings, leaving her with an intimate sense of connection to the author.

"Whose letter is this?" she asked, her voice reverent in the quiet bookstore.

The voice that responded belonged to a man who sat behind the counter with a warm smile and kind eyes. "Mine," he said. He introduced himself as Jake Powers, the bookstore's owner. A young woman he introduced as his wife, Natalie, sat beside him. They were the living embodiment of Bea's wish in the letter. The story of Bea and her daughter Brandy unfolded through Jake's words, leaving Amanda and Jackson engrossed and touched by a mother's love and the gift of life that extended beyond the physical realm.

"Your book is in the back, Jackson," Natalie said.

Jackson excused himself to pick up the book he'd ordered. As he disappeared into the maze of bookshelves, Amanda continued her conversation with Jake, asking him about his journey to Aspen Cove.

Under the soft glow of the bookstore's warm lighting. Jake, the bookstore's proprietor, shared how he'd never known Bea or Brandy personally but had been a recipient of one of Brandy's kidneys, and had been moved by the pink letter he'd received. Out of reverence, he had opened this bookstore in their honor, a quiet tribute to their giving spirits.

Amanda listened—her heartstrings plucked by the gentle narrative. A sense of kinship bloomed within her, heat spreading through her veins. She, too, was a recipient of Bea's far-reaching kindness. The cabin she now called home was proof of that.

A slow sigh slipped past Amanda's lips as she turned to Jake. "I knew Brandy, you know," she started, her voice a soft murmur in the hush of the bookstore. "We were pen pals when we were younger." She recounted how Brandy would always tuck hand-colored bookmarks into her letters, tiny tokens of kindness that spoke volumes of her sweet nature. She could almost see Brandy's bright smile and feel her laughter echoing through the room. The image made her heart ache with sweet sorrow, but the pain was a small price to pay for keeping Brandy's memory alive.

Amid the murmur of conversation and the rustle of turning pages, Jackson returned with a familiar book in his hands. The sight of Jane Austen's *Emma* made Amanda blink in surprise. "I didn't expect you to be a Jane Austen fan, Jackson."

His blush was charming, as warming as the crackling fire back at the cabin. "I'm not. But I knew she was your favorite, so I thought we could read it together." The sincerity in his voice tugged at her heart, turning the corners of her mouth into a wide smile.

As they left the bookstore, they carried more than just a book. They bore the spirit of kindness and love that was Brandy and Bea's legacy, a reminder of life's fleeting moments and the enduring power of human connection.

The hour-long drive to Copper Creek offered a spectacle of nature's grandeur, mountains reaching for the skies, cloaked in verdant green and dusted with snow.

The wind hummed, the tree's leaves whispering secrets to the sky. Now and then, Jackson would point out a landmark, his voice a soothing soundtrack to the breathtaking panorama outside the window.

Once they arrived in Copper Creek, the day unfolded in a flurry of activity. They bustled around the market, collecting supplies for the Thanksgiving feast. Amanda savored the familiar scents wafting from the fresh produce, the sweetness of ripe fruit and the earthiness of vegetables painting a fragrant canvas for the feast she was planning.

A sense of excitement bubbled within her as she picked up the ingredients for Bea's special ham. She could almost taste the succulent flavor, the memories of Bea infusing every morsel with a love that transcended time and loss.

After their shopping was done, Jackson turned to her with a boyish grin that made her heart do a little flip. "How about dinner at Trevi's Steakhouse?"

The suggestion surprised her, and she hesitated, catching her lower lip between her teeth. "Are you asking me on a date, Jackson?"

His response was immediate and sent a flutter through her chest. "Yes, I am."

At Trevi's, they found themselves lost in an intimate world of their own. The mouth-watering steak mingled with the sweet scent of burning wood, enveloping them in a cocoon of comfort. Their conversation flowed as easy as a mountain stream.

A shared dish of creamy mashed potatoes led to their hands brushing against each other. The contact was electric, a charge that coursed through them, leaving a lingering sense of connection and want.

Throughout their meal, a sense of heightened awareness persisted. Each word Jackson said was laced with a gentle innuendo that pulled her in like a magnet, their words filled with subtle hints and secret winks.

The thought of sharing dessert, a creamy, decadent chocolate mousse, promised more than just a sweet finish to their meal. Each glance exchanged over the shared treat spoke volumes, a silent understanding sealed with every taste savored from their spoons.

The taste of the bittersweet and rich mousse was nothing compared to the charged atmosphere between them. The way Jackson's eyes tracked her as she savored the dessert was more intoxicating than the wine. And when he licked his spoon, a hint of chocolate on his lips, it was all she could do to remain seated.

Under the table, his foot brushed against hers. It was accidental, just a shift of his weight, but the connection sent jolts up her spine that pooled in her core. The touch hinted at what was to come, a temptation that urged her to explore further.

The drive back was pure torture. Every shared glance, every unspoken word, was filled with promise. Their interaction at dinner had shifted something and altered the chemistry between them. As they pulled up to the cabin, both knew they were on the cusp of something electric, an exploration of longing as sweet as the mousse they had shared.

The moment the truck parked, a breathless silence took over. A moment suspended in time strung between what was and what would be.

Jackson turned off the engine, but neither moved. They remained seated in the warm cab, the sounds of the night seeping in through the closed windows. The rustling of the wind through the trees, the hoot of an owl somewhere in the distance, and the occasional crunch of leaves under the feet of night critters.

Without uttering a word, he reached out to tuck a loose strand of hair behind her ear. His touch lingered, tracing the curve of her ear, trailing down to rest on her shoulder. Her breath hitched. She could feel the heat of his palm through her sweater, a comforting pressure that was at once grounding and exhilarating.

In the privacy of the truck, away from the world's prying eyes, she turned toward him. Their faces were close. She could see the flecks of gold in his eyes.

His hand moved from her shoulder, trailing down her arm to catch her hand in his. He lifted it, pressing a soft kiss on her knuckles. It was a simple gesture, but it left heat coursing through her veins, leaving her breathless.

"Let's go inside," he suggested in a whisper, as if afraid to break the enchanting spell woven around them.

Nodding, she followed him out of the truck, up the steps, and into the cabin.

Inside, their shared space seemed different. Every corner was laden with a new meaning and a feeling of expectation. The living room where they'd shared countless conversations now seemed to hold a different purpose altogether. The couch, their bedrooms—all paled in significance to what was about to happen.

Jackson was the first to break the silence. "Amanda," he whispered, his voice rough with a raw need mirroring her own. The sound of her name on his lips was a sweet melody, sending shivers down her spine. He reached out to her, pulling her closer, his eyes never leaving hers.

When their lips met, it was like the culmination of every shared smile, every stolen glance, every innuendo-filled conversation. The kiss was a delicious exploration, a slow dance that swept them off their feet.

He pulled back. "More?"

She wasn't sure if it was a question or a request, and it didn't matter. All she could do was nod.

Seconds later, they found themselves in her bedroom, their clothes discarded in a trail that led to her bed. The heat of his flesh against hers was like liquid fire, filling her with a desire that stretched through her body. Her nipples hardened, and a deep longing settled between her legs.

His lips traveled down the length of her neck, finding the sensitive spots that made her moan out loud. She lifted to meet his tongue as he explored further—kissing and licking every inch of her body until she trembled beneath him.

He seemed to know every place to touch that took her closer and closer to the edge.

She gasped at the new sensation and arched into him as his fingers caressed and teased until she could no longer take it. "Please," she begged.

He responded by pushing himself deep inside her—thrusting slowly and steadily into the depths of her being until all thought fell away, and they moved together as one. Every movement heightened their pleasure until it reached its peak with an explosion of light and ecstasy that left them both trembling in its wake.

Jackson's deep voice reverberated through the quiet room as they lay entangled in the soft linen sheets. "I'm glad I found you," he murmured, his fingers tracing patterns on her back.

A chuckle bubbled from her throat. Her voice was tired yet playful. "Oh, you found me? If I recall correctly, I was already at the cabin when you showed up."

Jackson's low laugh echoed in the dark room, making her heart flutter. "Fair point," he conceded, his tone light and teasing. "Then we can agree that it's good we found each other."

A comfortable silence settled around them, filled only by their soft breaths and the beating of two hearts drawing closer in the quiet darkness. It was a declaration of more than just shared desire; it was an acknowledgment of a bond that had formed, a bond that was beginning to feel a lot like love.

CHAPTER SIXTEEN

Days had passed since that blissful night, a series of sunrises and sunsets. Each day, they woke in each other's arms, pulling them closer together. He'd rise before her to feed the animals and make coffee. She'd get up shortly after to help make breakfast. They'd sit together and discuss their day, with him tackling a project in the cabin before he went to work at the brewhouse. Amanda had a cup of coffee or two before she'd sit at the desk by the window and marvel at how perfect that tree in her yard was, but days ago, she stopped calling it her yard and started to refer to it as theirs which always filled him to the brim with joy.

When she emerged that morning, her brown hair a tangled mess and a sleepy smile on her face, she was a sight to behold. His heart stilled, and his breath hitched. It was a daily reminder of his growing feelings. She caught his gaze, then smiled. Ground coffee beans and fresh morning air filled the cabin. The scent was a comforting ritual, a sensory echo of their shared moments. Her fingers brushed against his when she accepted the steaming mug. An electric jolt shot up his arm, a reaction that had become a common occurrence each time she touched him.

One of Jackson's newfound pleasures was cooking together in the cabin. Their camaraderie and chemistry were undeniable.

"What can I help with?"

She leaned against the counter, lined with Bea's ham ingredients that didn't require refrigeration. "Are you done with the tree?"

He nodded. "Put that last strand of lights up yesterday."

"Maybe we should have bought new lights."

Jackson shook his head. "Nope, it's important that we used what everyone offered." He took an assortment of donated lights from the residents and strung them together to decorate the Christmas tree he'd secured in the town square. It wasn't an actual town square but more of a center of a roundabout with several benches that faced a patch of dead grass, but he had to admit that Katie's vision for its transformation was nothing short of genius. It was as if the space was always meant to have a big tree, and the twelve-footer he cut down was perfect. "All it needs are decorations and people. Doc is going to do the honors and flip the switch."

Amanda smiled. "I love how everyone comes together to pitch in. The world could learn something from Aspen Cove." She pointed to a box by the tree. "I set aside a few of Bea's more durable ornaments for us to bring."

"That's very thoughtful of you." He wrapped his arms around her and hugged her tightly. "Now, how can I help with the feast?"

Amanda's decision to cook Bea's ham for the Thanksgiving feast came naturally. Bea's memory echoed in Aspen Cove's collective consciousness, and even though Jackson and Amanda hadn't personally known her, they recognized the significance of her contribution to the town. Without Bea, he wouldn't have met Amanda. Without Bea, the cabin would be vacant except for the resident raccoon, who often knocked on the door as if asking to reenter. If not for Bea, the town would still be dying rather than thriving with new residents that Bea had handpicked to bring it back to life. They were cooking not just a ham but a symbol of unity, a token of love that Bea had once embodied.

"Let's start here." She pointed to the original recipe, handwritten by Bea herself. The recipe card was more than a list of ingredients and steps; it was a ticket into the past, a tangible thread that tied the townsfolk to the woman.

Amanda traced her fingers over the worn-out letters, her smile both wistful and respectful. "We need to do justice to this, Jackson."

Meeting her gaze, he nodded. "We will."

And so, they embarked on their culinary adventure together, an invisible beat guiding them as they worked side by side. The slicing of vegetables, the careful glazing of the ham, the familiar sounds of simmering sauces, and the popping and sizzling from the stove.

With each passing hour, as the ham slowly roasted in the oven, the cabin was filled with a tantalizing smell. It was sweet and savory, a smell that permeated every corner, curled around each piece of furniture, and seeped into their clothes. As Jackson tended to the ham, basting it one final time before it was ready, Amanda's hand rested gently on his shoulder. He turned to find her standing close, her eyes reflecting the same thoughts swirling in his mind. She squeezed him, her smile reassuring. "We did good, Jackson." She kissed him. "We've got an hour to spare. Whatever shall we do?" She looked toward the hallway.

He didn't need an invitation. "I'll beat you there." He lowered the temperature of the oven and dashed for the bedroom.

THE GUILD CREATIVE Center was bustling with activity, a hive of excitement echoing with laughter and the murmur of conversation. Streamers hung from the rafters, and tables lined with festive tablecloths held a vast spread of dishes brought in by the residents. The smell of home-cooked meals permeated the air—the savory scent of roasted meats, the sweetness of pies, and the rich yeastiness of warm bread.

Jackson and Amanda entered, a warm roasting pan between them. "I don't think anyone will notice we're late," Jackson said as they found a place on the table for their contribution.

The chatter dimmed as Doc rose to his feet. His presence commanded attention, a demonstration to the respect he held in the hearts of Aspen Cove residents. Jackson's heart rate slowed as he focused on the older man, who was a father to all.

"We gather here, a symbol of our unity and resilience. We've weathered many storms, some real, others metaphorical," Doc began, his voice rich with emotion. "And today, we honor one of our own who isn't with us anymore—Bea."

A hush fell over the room at the mention of Bea's name. Jackson felt the memories of the woman he'd never met but had come to respect surge in the minds of the people around him.

"Bea, with her spirit and dedication, brought many new faces to Aspen Cove. Faces that have now become part of our family," Doc continued, his gaze finding Jackson's. It was an acknowledgment of his place in the town, a place he'd come to call home.

Amanda squeezed his hand, her heat seeping into his skin, grounding him, reinforcing the sense of belonging. The corners of his mouth twitched upward in a small smile.

Doc's words resonated within him. This was what he'd hoped for when he'd arrived. He wanted to be a part of something like a family and as he glanced at Amanda, he saw the possibility for that to happen.

"Without Bea, we might've seen the end of our little town. But look at us now." Doc spread his arms, taking in the bustling room, the array of dishes, and the people. "We continue to grow, to thrive. Because of her and because of us. We are Aspen Cove, and as long as we stand together, our town will never fade away."

The applause that followed was heartfelt, a cacophony of claps that echoed through the room. A sense of unity filled the space, as powerful as the chill outside, as potent as his connection with Amanda.

Jackson glanced at her. Together, they were part of this place, this family. This was their home, and they would do everything to keep it alive and thriving.

The Thanksgiving feast resumed, filled with joy, camaraderie, and deep appreciation for the town, for Bea and each other. Jackson could not help but feel a stirring of excitement for what was to come: the tree lighting, the holidays, and his gift to the town that had made him feel welcome.

They all grabbed plates and filled them with everything from Bea's homemade ham to Bobby Williams's turducken.

The center was like a picture postcard of the perfect holiday. The town's residents gathered in clusters, engaging in conversation, sharing stories, laughter echoing around the room.

Amid it all, Amanda was like a ray of sunshine, her cheer adding to the harmony. She greeted each person, her charm seeping into the atmosphere and endearing her to them instantly.

Jackson leaned against a wall, his eyes trailing Amanda as she mingled with the crowd. She conversed with Tilden, the town's lumberjack, his laughter booming in response to something she'd said. She seemed genuinely interested, her brown eyes alight with curiosity as she asked him about his work, family, and life in Aspen Cove.

Next, she moved to Goldie, Tilden's wife, and the town's social influencer. Goldie's radiant smile widened at the sight of Amanda, the two of them falling into easy conversation as they shared a plate of pumpkin pie. Amanda's nose wrinkled when she laughed at something Goldie said. The sight tugged at Jackson's heart. He saw a little girl with brown eyes in their future.

Jackson watched her interact with Trinity and Wyatt, two ranchers who worked on Abby's property. He could hear her questions about their journey to the area and what they found here that they couldn't find elsewhere.

She then moved on to Riley and Luke. They entertained her with how they met when Riley nearly burned down the Guild Creative Center and Luke had to put the fire out. But luckily, they still smoldered for each other.

She dove into the history of the residents, showing a genuine interest in their lives. He realized that she wasn't just meeting them. She was interviewing them for parts of her own story, which was unfolding daily.

After the feast, the townsfolk cleaned up and moved to the town square, where the tree he'd cut stood tall and majestic under the clear night sky. The cold night frosted his cheeks, but he hardly noticed, because his heart was pounding so hard. The residents approached, each carrying an ornament in their hands and a sparkle in their eyes that mirrored the twinkling stars above.

The Christmas tree, the centerpiece, was a symbol of what they built together. Its branches reached out, strong and inviting, ready to embrace the tokens of love and memories each ornament represented. Under the glow of the moon and stars, it stood bare but beautiful, like a canvas waiting to be painted with the colors of their shared experiences.

Amanda's hand slipped into his, their fingers intertwining as they approached the tree. They had chosen their ornament, a delicate glass snowflake glinting in the moonlight. The residents stepped forward, each hanging their decorations on a tree branch. Tilden hung a mini saw ornament, a tribute to his work as the local firewood supplier. Goldie placed a miniature phone ornament, a reflection of her passion. Trinity and Wyatt chose horse figurines, evidence of their love for their work at the ranch. Riley and Luke hung an original forged by Riley. Sosie hung a mini painting, while Eden, another town resident, hung a baby Jesus. Everyone brought something that reflected who they were to the town. There were wrenches, books, flowers, glass bacon, plastic crayons, and a pair of mismatched socks from Peter. Every resident was represented, and each ornament added a unique charm to the tree. It was transformed from a plain fir into a vibrant emblem of unity, its branches laden with tokens of love.

Finally, it was their turn. With Amanda's hand still tucked securely in his, they stepped forward, the excitement coursing through them as he lifted their glass snowflake, its surface catching the moonlight and scattering it like a prism. He hung it on a branch, the snowflake swinging as it found its place amongst the other ornaments. It seemed fitting, as a storm was what brought them together. A raccoon would have worked, too, but there were no such critters in Bea's treasures.

As he stepped back, he could feel a sense of accomplishment. His gaze lingered on the snowflake before drifting to the woman beside him, her face illuminated under the moonlight, her eyes shimmering with unspoken emotions.

The town square was abuzz with a shared sense of excitement. The low murmur of the crowd ebbed away as Doc stepped toward the Christmas tree. Everyone's faces were lit by the light of the moon and the twinkling stars above.

The crowd's pulse seemed like a collective heartbeat that thrummed in sync with his own. At his side, Gunner sat obediently, his eyes alert and watchful. The dog's warm, furry presence against his leg was a comforting constant in the whirlwind of emotions he was feeling.

Doc's finger traced over the switch. This moment, the lighting of the tree, was a first for the town, but Jackson hoped it would be a tradition that would be celebrated for years to come.

The crowd held its breath. Time seemed to pause as Doc flipped the switch. A hush descended, the night's silence amplifying the town's heartbeat.

Jackson squeezed Amanda's hand. Gunner shifted at his side. The dog's attentive gaze fixed on the tree. The moment had come. It was a memory he knew would be etched deep within the heart of the town, a story that would be retold for years to come. This was his gift to everyone.

The tree erupted into a dazzling array of lights, illuminating the town square, and reflecting off the awed faces of everyone. A gasp swept through the crowd, a wave of delighted exclamations echoing in the night. The brilliance of the lights cast long shadows across the square, the vibrant colors bathing everything in a cheerful glow.

Gunner growled low in his throat; his gaze fixed on the tree. Jackson followed the dog's line of sight, his breath hitching as he spotted the telltale glow at the tree's base. The spark that was supposed to herald joy and unity was, instead, a harbinger of disaster.

His grip tightened around Amanda's hand as the glow intensified, a small flame licking up the side of the tree. "Fire..." he whispered. But it was loud enough. Loud enough for Amanda to hear, loud enough for the word to spread a ripple of panic through the crowd.

In the face of disaster, the beauty of the lights became a cruel irony, a symbol of his failure. The joyous cries turned into gasps of horror as the flames grew, greedily consuming the tree he'd put up.

Aiden Cooper pushed everyone back as the local fire department came to the rescue and doused the flames.

His gaze found Amanda among the sea of shocked faces. Her ordinarily vibrant eyes were wide, her mouth open as she alternated between looking at the tree and back at him. Her hand tightened around his in an attempt to lend comfort, but he found none. The bitter taste of failure consumed him. Gunner whimpered at his side, his intense gaze fixed on the charred remains. The shepherd's unease mirrored his own, the despair seeping into his marrow. He bent down, scratching Gunner's ears in a small act of kindness in the chaos.

Amanda, her hand a steady presence in his, looked at

him. Her eyes were full of concern but not blame. "We can fix this," she said.

His mind seized on her words. Fix this? The tree was a charred skeleton. The ashes of the ornaments fluttered around them like grim snowflakes. He'd shattered a precious heirloom, the fragments too tiny and numerous to piece back together.

"This can't be fixed." His gaze was still on the smoldering remnants of the tree. "I've destroyed everything. You were right. We shouldn't have used those lights."

CHAPTER SEVENTEEN

The silence stretched around Amanda as she and Jackson drove back to their cabin. The inky expanse of the night sky was shrouded in an uneasy quiet. The occasional call of a distant creature interrupted the otherwise quiet drive, filling Amanda with unease.

Jackson, who was usually full of cheerfulness, was unnervingly silent. His demeanor had darkened, mirroring the desolate winter landscape around them. As she stole a sideways glance, his downturned face was a sight that pained her, his eyes reflecting a sadness she'd never seen in them before.

The dimly lit windows appeared as welcoming eyes in the cold night as they approached. The chimney exhaled soft plumes of smoke from the earlier banked fire. However, this warm refuge she called home seemed a touch colder tonight.

Once inside, Jackson removed his jacket and boots in an almost robotic manner. It was as if his mind was wrestling with his thoughts. The embers from the fireplace cast him in a glow. The smell from the burning wood would usually soothe Amanda, but it only accentuated her loneliness tonight.

Jackson spoke, breaking the silence that had trailed them into the cabin. "I don't know what they will think of me now. I should have listened to you about the lights." An uncertain tremor replaced his confident tone. The people he spoke of, the folks in Aspen Cove, had, until this mishap, been welcoming. The prospect of losing their acceptance was visibly eating at him. "I messed up," he admitted, the words seeming to leave an awful taste in his mouth as he spat them out. "Finally, I belonged somewhere ... with them, with you. And now, I've ruined everything by ruining Christmas and Thanksgiving by association."

Amanda, filled with empathy, crossed the room to him. She held his cold hands in hers, trying to warm them, to reassure him. "Jackson," she began, her voice full of tenderness, "you're not the Grinch who stole Christmas. The residents of Aspen Cove donated those lights, and one strand was bad. It was a collective effort, so the responsibility is shared too. This isn't on you. Your heart was in the right place."

She truly believed in the community spirit. If anyone could understand a mistake born from good intentions, it would be them. She hoped her words would kindle the same belief in Jackson, however, she knew that her warning about the lights would be all he remembered.

Despite Amanda's reassurances, Jackson's guilt remained like a heavy shadow across his face. He met her eyes with an expression mingling thankfulness and sorrow. "I appreciate what you're trying to do," he whispered. "But I just ... I need some time to think. I need to figure out what I'm going to do."

He kissed her forehead before retreating to his room,

with Gunner following close behind. The echo of the door closing reverberated through the cabin. Alone in the silence, she recognized that Jackson's guilt prevented him from seeing the compassion and understanding the people would have for him.

She realized then that words, however comforting, wouldn't alleviate Jackson's guilt. Action was required. As she sat by the dying fire, she was consumed by thoughts of how she could help him realize that he wasn't responsible and that they could restore the holiday spirit. If she didn't, there was a chance that she'd lose him.

The first blush of morning found Amanda pulling on her coat, ready to venture into town. When she peeked inside his door, Jackson was still asleep, his face drawn into a tight mask that showed the unrest plaguing him. She wanted to be there for him, but the conversation last night had made one thing clear: words, normally her superpower, were not enough. She had to demonstrate the kindness and compassion that she wanted the people of Aspen Cove to show.

Closing the door, she stepped into the cold morning air and took a moment to look at the perfect tree standing tall in her yard. Under the first light of morning, it held a mystic aura, its branches heavy with snow, gleaming with a sprinkling of frost.

THE TOWN WAS COMING to life as she reached Main Street. Looking over her shoulder toward the town square, she could see the charred remains of the second-prettiest tree ever.

She glanced around and saw that the pharmacy light

was on, meaning Doc had to be up. She hoped he was ready for her. Known for his wit and wisdom, she walked inside, hoping to get some advice, but she found Agatha at the register.

"Welcome in. Are you looking for something in particular?"

Amanda nodded. "I need advice."

Agatha smiled. "If it's love advice, I'm probably your girl. You'll have to speak to Doc if it's how to get rid of a rash in your nether regions."

"No rash. It's about a man but not a love problem."

Agatha knitted her brows together. "When the topic is a man, it typically pertains to love."

She hadn't considered love, yet that was the undeniable truth. She certainly had a problem. She was in love with Jackson Knight, and if he left Aspen Cove, he'd take his love with him, and she'd be left with a broken heart. "You're right, I love him, but our love isn't the problem. It's the whole tree-lighting debacle, and I need some advice."

Agatha shook her head. "I know nothing about trees."

Before Amanda could say it wasn't about the tree, Agatha walked over to the stairs and called for Doc to come down. After several minutes, a *clump, clump* sound announced Doc Parker's arrival. When he reached the bottom step, he pointed to the office down the hall.

She walked in front of him, not knowing where to go, but she found only one door open and walked inside.

Doc took his stethoscope from the counter and wrapped it around the back of his neck.

"What ails you today?" He nodded to the exam table.

Rather than argue, she climbed up. "It's not medical. I need advice on how to cheer up Jackson."

Doc rolled his eyes. "You two having a spat already?"

"No, it's not us. You were there last night and saw what happened."

Doc chuckled. "Best town bonfire since Riley set fire to the Guild Creative Center and Samantha's agent burned her house to the ground."

Amanda's eyes went wide. "What?"

"Yep, you newcomers bring a lot of excitement."

"I haven't burned anything down."

Doc took a seat in the corner. "Not yet." He rubbed his bushy mustache. "What's wrong with Jackson?"

"He's blaming himself."

"You want me to go up to your place and slap him upside the head?"

"Do you think it would work?"

Doc kicked out his feet. "Probably not." His black sneakers had seen better days, but Amanda imagined they were comfortable and that's why Doc wore them. Aspen Cove was like an old pair of shoes to Jackson, but now he wasn't sure if they'd still fit.

"He's afraid he won't be accepted in town now that he burned down the tree."

"He didn't burn the tree down. It was an accident."

"I know, and I told him that, but he's convinced everyone will look at him differently. Saying it doesn't matter doesn't mean it's true. Right now, words have no power."

Doc stared at her for a minute. "That must be difficult for you being a wordsmith and all. Words are your currency, and you can't cash in." He stared at the wall. "Seems to me that actions always speak louder than words."

"You're right, but I'm new here. Who will listen to me?"

"That's the thing with small towns, everyone is listening. You need to get the message to the right people."

"The problem is, I don't know what the message is. I can't tell everyone that Jackson is depressed. That seems like a betrayal."

Doc rose. "I can't help you there. Sounds like you need a brownie."

"A brownie?"

He nodded and started to walk toward the door. "The best way to get an idea to take root is with Katie's famous brownies," he said before leaving.

"What do I owe you?"

He laughed. "If you ever write about me, I want people to think I look like Sam Elliot when he was in his forties and fifties."

She laughed. "Got it." She waved to Agatha and walked out of the pharmacy. She didn't have a solution, but she wouldn't mind a brownie.

Katie's shop stood at the corner. Its window display was filled with festive decorations that sparked a sense of cheer despite the disaster last night. The bell jingled as Amanda entered, drawing Katie's attention.

"Amanda," Katie greeted, concern evident in her voice. "How's Jackson?"

Amanda gave a small smile, her gaze wandering toward The Wishing Wall. "He's ... struggling."

"I can imagine."

"I don't know what to do. Doc told me to come here and have a brownie, and an idea will take root."

"Doc's rarely wrong." Katie plated a brownie and delivered it to the table under The Wishing Wall.

Amanda took a bite of the brownie and thought about Doc's words, and an idea sparked. She reached out to grab a pen and a small piece of paper. Her heart pounded as she wrote down her wish, a silent prayer on her lips. She stuck it to the board and stepped back.

Katie leaned in to see what Amanda had written. "I wish someone would dig up the perfect tree from our yard and replant it in the town square," Katie read aloud, her eyebrows shooting up in surprise. "Are you serious?"

"I am."

Katie cocked her head. "But when I was out there, you said you'd never give the tree up."

Amanda remembered that day all too well. "They say never say never. And sometimes, never turns into maybe, and yes, when the timing is right, or the need is great. Besides, I don't want to cut it down. I want to transplant it. It seems a shame to kill something so lovely."

"That's a big wish. It's winter, and transplanting will shock it."

Amanda nodded. "I know, but I think ... it's what the town needs. What Jackson needs."

Katie stared at her. "That tree is perfect, sure. But..."

Amanda thought about Jackson, who'd taught her that some experiences were better when not faced alone. She considered the moments they'd shared, which felt all the more remarkable because they were together.

"But nothing. When you came to my house and asked about the tree, I didn't understand what Aspen Cove was about, and now I do," Amanda answered, her voice firm. "Things are better when shared. Friendship. Love. A tree. Responsibility. Jackson taught me that. And now, I think it's time we taught him the same."

Katie studied her, the sincerity in her gaze matching her own. She nodded, her lips curling into a small smile. "You're right. And you know what? I think I can make it happen."

Amanda left the shop, and a new hope blossomed in her heart. The magic of the season was still very much alive.

When she returned, she found Jackson in the kitchen, a steaming cup of coffee in his hands. His posture was hunched, the morning light casting long shadows on his face. Yet, when he looked up and met her gaze, there was a certain clarity in his eyes that hadn't been there the night before.

"Hey," he said, his voice a soft balm to her worries. "I owe you an apology."

She blinked in surprise, reaching out her hand to rest on his arm. His skin was warm, a big difference from the cold morning outside.

"For last night," he explained. "I shouldn't have left you alone. That was ... selfish of me."

She studied him for a moment, her heart warming at his words. She realized then he wasn't just battling his guilt over the town's Christmas lights. He was also wrestling with the guilt of shutting her out and letting his shame and embarrassment overwhelm him to the point that he'd left her to bear the weight alone.

He ran a hand through his hair, a nervous gesture she'd come to recognize. "I don't know how I'm ever going to walk through town again," he admitted. "But that's my cross to bear. I shouldn't have made you suffer too."

She shook her head. "Jackson, you don't have to bear anything alone. Not in this town. Not with me."

He leaned in and kissed her. "I missed you last night," he murmured against her lips, his voice filled with regret and affection.

His confession stirred something within her that seeped deep into her bones. "I missed you too," she said.

"Do you need to work right now?"

"No, I just want to be with you." She thought about telling him her plan but decided to wait in case it didn't work out. "Why?"

"Because I have a night to make up for." With a soft pull, he led her toward her bedroom. As the door closed behind them, the outside world was a million miles away.

CHAPTER EIGHTEEN

The interior of the cabin was scented with the rich smell of just-made coffee and sharp, clean pine. Jackson was deep in his task, methodically dragging the wood plane over the bare boards. His strong muscles worked in a pattern of familiarity, transforming the rough surface into a smooth one with expert hands.

Meanwhile, the fireplace popped and crackled, casting lively shadows over the cabin's rustic features. Gunner was stretched out near the heat, his ears flicking in his sleep and his tail lazily thumping against the floor. Catsby lounged on the sunny window ledge, his vibrant fur ablaze in the soft daylight.

Across the room from Jackson, Amanda was nestled in the comfy armchair near the fireplace, immersed in her writing project. Her face held a focused intensity, pencil sweeping over the pages with practiced grace. She'd nibble on the end of her pencil, her brow creasing as she navigated through her thoughts. He'd become quite fond of this sight, admiring how her eyes lit up when she was buried in her creativity. She wouldn't tell him anything about the story, only that he'd like it when she was finished.

The peaceful moment was interrupted by a familiar buzz. Amanda's cell phone lit up on the coffee table, the screen announcing a new message. Jackson looked up from his task, his eyes resting on her as a surprised smile painted her face, her eyes widening as she processed the message's contents. The thud of her pencil dropping onto her book echoed in the silent room. "Jackson," she called, capturing his attention.

He placed the wood plane down, his eyes meeting hers. "Yeah? What's up?"

"Would you mind if we made a trip to Copper Creek? I want to get some Christmas lights."

Jackson raised an eyebrow, stunned by the sudden shift in their plans. "Christmas lights?" he echoed, pushing himself upright. The wooden planks under his feet protested.

"Yes," she said. "I've been thinking about decorating the tree in our yard. I think it's time we invited some holiday cheer to our neck of the woods, wouldn't you agree?"

"We already have the tree inside all lit up." Considering the previous unfortunate incident, he was hesitant about dressing up another tree outside.

"I know," she responded, "but wouldn't it be amazing to have another one outside?"

"I know what you're doing. You're trying to create a do-over for the last disaster, but it won't work."

"Stop being a party pooper. No one is blaming you."

He frowned. "It's because I haven't been in town in almost a week." He'd never been a coward, but he figured the longer he stayed away, the more likely the townsfolk would forget.

"Please." She steepled her hands as if in prayer and that was his undoing. He couldn't deny her. "Alright," he conceded, a small smile pulling at the corners of his lips as he dusted his hands off on his work jeans. "Let's do it." He crossed the room to join her, causing Catsby to leap off his spot and Gunner to lazily lift his head to survey the change.

Amanda set her notebook and pencil on the chair after standing up. They faced each other, only a breath of space separating them. Their eyes locked, mirroring their affection. Amanda tipped onto her toes, her fingers threading around Jackson's shirt as she coaxed him closer. Their lips connected in a tender, lingering kiss that stirred a rush of emotion.

After pulling back, they kept their foreheads resting against each other, their breaths merging in the center. A moment of comfortable silence wrapped them, emphasizing the depth of their shared connection. Amanda released him before fetching her jacket from the coat stand. Her lips were still curled in a contented smile. "This will be so much fun."

After casting a final look at his unfinished work, Jackson ensured the fire was banked and the screen was in place before he followed suit. He bent down to ruffle Gunner's soft fur, whispering a quick "be good" before waving a playful farewell to the aloof Catsby. With a final glance at the room, he followed Amanda outside and closed the cabin door behind them.

The pickup engine rumbled to life, a low and comforting purr that vibrated beneath them. The truck was much like Jackson himself—rugged, dependable, and filled with a quiet strength that was undeniable. At least, that was how he thought people once saw him.

They made their way down the country road to the

highway. The route, framed by the snowy landscape and distant mountains, was almost magical. Above them, a hawk made lazy circles in the sky, its piercing eyes scanning the ground below. A deer flashed across the road and vanished into the thick brush.

Amanda broke the silence, her voice soft but laced with concern. "You haven't been to the bar in days, Jackson. You can't keep hiding." The words hung in the air between them.

They drove silently for a few seconds before Jackson responded, his voice gruff. "Cannon gave me a few days off when I said I needed time." He glanced over at her, looking for some understanding.

She nodded. "That was considerate of him."

"Yeah," he agreed, a heavy sigh escaping his lips. "I guess ... I guess I'm just scared. What happened wasn't intentional, but I can't shake off the feeling that folks are blaming me."

She reached over and gave his hand a gentle squeeze. "Jackson, people aren't always as harsh as we make them out to be in our heads. Sometimes, they're just concerned, not blaming."

"But—"

She cut him off. "What happened was an accident. And everyone knows that. You're punishing yourself more than anyone else is."

He fell silent, letting her words sink in. Maybe she was right—he was unable to forgive himself, projecting his guilt onto others. It wasn't easy, but perhaps facing the people and moving forward was the right thing to do. The problem was he wasn't sure he was ready for that.

"You're probably right."

The drive led them into Copper Creek, a much larger

town, busier than Aspen Cove and fully decked out for the holidays. Christmas lights shone from every building, illuminating the streets in festive colors. Shop windows displayed various Christmas merchandise, each more enticing than the last.

Their first stop was The Glittering Fir. They stepped inside and were met with a rush of holiday cheer. Christmas songs played in the background while shoppers moved through the store eagerly. Every step brought a stronger smell of pine and cinnamon, no doubt from the garland strung around the entryway and candles that burned in pretty glass jars. It was like Christmas had already arrived.

Amanda seemed to shine in this environment. She moved from aisle to aisle, her fingers brushing over shimmering ornaments and strands of lights. She was like a kid in a candy store, and Jackson found joy in just watching her.

"Jackson," she called, waving two strands of Christmas lights at him—one cool blue, the other warm gold. "Which one would look better on our tree?"

He took a moment to look at her eyes sparkling with happiness before shrugging. "Whichever one keeps that smile on your face." At that moment, surrounded by the festive cheer, Jackson realized that his worries about returning to Aspen Cove paled in comparison to the joy he was experiencing right now, just being with Amanda. They bought warm gold lights.

After The Glittering Fir, they visited several other shops. Each was decked out for the holidays with various decorations, filling the air with sweet treats and peppermint scents. Amanda guided Jackson through each shop, considering the items and often asking for his opinion. Her enthusiasm entertained him, and he enjoyed the experience more than expected.

ONE HUNDRED MERRY MEMORIES

They spent the morning shopping, and the lively energy of the city left them feeling excited rather than tired. When lunchtime came around, Amanda suggested they find a place to eat. They chose a small café decorated with white lights and green garlands.

Inside, the café was warm and smelled of coffee and fresh bread. Soft jazz played in the background, creating an engaging and comfortable atmosphere. They sat by the window, watching the bustling town while they ate and chatted. Their conversation flowed easily, filled with shared laughs and stories.

Just as they were finishing lunch, Amanda got a text. After reading it, she seemed eager to get going. "Ready to head back?" she asked, looking toward the door. Although it was a sudden change, Jackson agreed. They picked up their shopping bags and headed back to their truck, ready to make their way home.

"I need to stop in town for a moment."

Jackson frowned but nodded.

When they returned to Aspen Cove, he noticed a lot of activity in the town square. The place was packed, with people laughing and looking excited. Jackson was nervous, surprised by the unexpected crowd.

"Amanda, what's happening?" he asked, his voice shaky. He looked around at the crowd, bracing for harsh looks, but all he saw were friendly smiles and waves.

"You'll see," Amanda said, giving him a mysterious smile. "Let's park."

"But..." Though he was reticent to follow her directions, he pulled into a free space and parked the truck. This time she beat him out of the truck and rushed around to his door, opening it, and offering him her hand.

Her grip was solid and reassuring. He started to feel a little less worried and a bit curious.

"Grab the bags we bought."

Everyone in the square got quiet and turned toward them. Jackson held his breath as he got the decorations from the truck.

Then he saw it.

In the middle of the square was a tree. But it wasn't just any tree but the giant spruce from Amanda's yard. He was stunned, his mind trying to understand what he was seeing. He was shocked, confused, and relieved all at once.

He looked at Amanda, who was grinning. "Surprise," she said, her eyes brimming with tears. Jackson let out a breath he didn't know he'd been holding. He still couldn't believe what was happening.

Looking at the tree again, he saw it in a new way. It wasn't just a tree anymore. It was a symbol of hope and new beginnings and a sign of the strength of their bond. The kindness and forgiveness the people of Aspen Cove had shown him was overwhelming. They had given him another chance, and he was ready to take it.

In the sea of eager faces, a familiar one caught Jackson's attention. Dressed in her vibrant red winter coat, Katie started walking toward them. Her expression was filled with purpose, a sight that intrigued and worried him simultaneously.

"Jackson, Amanda," Katie greeted them, her tone radiating excitement. She gestured toward the giant spruce with a wide grin. "We needed a new tree, and Amanda here had a perfect one."

Confusion filled him. He glanced at Amanda. "But it was perfect where it was."

With a soft squeeze of his hand, she turned to him. "I

made a wish, Jackson. I wanted our tree to bring joy to everyone in Aspen Cove. It belongs here."

His heart pounded, realization dawning on him. The Wishing Wall. The secret trips to town. The sudden text messages. It all made sense now.

"But ... how?" he managed to stammer out. Moving a tree that size was no small feat, especially in the heart of winter.

"With a lot of help and a little bit of hope," Katie chimed in. "We hired an arborist, dug it out, and brought it here. Given the shock of being uprooted and relocated, we had to stake it to support it."

Katie's gaze drifted toward the tree. Her smile was tinged with worry. "He said there's no guarantee it'll survive... The timing, the weather, it's not ideal."

Amanda's response was immediate, her words spoken with a faith that left him in awe. "Katie, all things thrive when planted and grown with love."

He could only watch, a lump in his throat, as the rest of the townsfolk approached them. Their hands were filled with strands of new Christmas lights, their faces reflecting the forgiveness and acceptance that their gesture implied.

They plugged them in strand by strand, to make sure everything was in order. With the lights in his hands and the people of Aspen Cove around him, Jackson was speechless. He glanced at Amanda, her eyes reflecting the warm glow of the Christmas lights.

"But I thought you loved that tree," he said, his voice filled with emotion.

She smiled at him, her words resonating through the chilly air. "I do, Jackson. But I love you more."

His heart stopped and then started with a bang as her words repeated in his mind. "You ... you love me?"

CHAPTER NINETEEN

"Yes," Amanda replied quietly, surprising herself with the certainty in her voice. "I do." Her confession was lost to the wind yet heard by the one person it was intended for.

Jackson's face transitioned from shock to disbelief to a soft smile that made her heart flutter. His eyes warmed with newfound understanding, a clarity that even she was still grappling with. She loved him. She had recognized his strength almost instantly—a silent, unyielding resilience that had seen him through the worst of times. His features, carved from experiences she could only imagine, told a tale of endurance and survival. It was a strength not just of body but of spirit, honed by adversity and trials she knew were part of his past. The thought of the horrors he'd faced, the life he'd led during the chaos of war as a soldier, made her admire him even more. He had weathered countless storms, each leaving its mark, shaping him into the man he was now—a man who, despite all odds, managed to love and be loved.

She'd seen the tenderness with which he treated the

people he cared about, his dedication unwavering and selfless.

He was strong but also full of laughter and good-natured humor that had a way of sneaking past her defenses. It was a potent combination that stirred something in her that she couldn't quite name.

Reaching up, she touched his face, his stubble prickling against her fingertips. Leaning in, she said, "You are kind and patient, handsome and strong." She tugged him down so her lips were next to his ear. "You're also an excellent lover." She stepped back and a blush spread from his neck to his ears. It was unexpected, a sweet testament to the man beneath the tough exterior.

"I'm glad you think so."

"I don't think ... I know."

Hand in hand, they stepped into the crowd that had gathered around the massive spruce tree. A cheer rose as they approached, the townsfolk encouraging Jackson to take the honor of hanging the lights on the tree. He glanced back at her with a sheepish smile as he shrugged off his jacket and rolled up his sleeves.

Thomas and the rest of his fire crew stood nearby, just in case.

"Come on, Jackson! You can do it!" Maisey shouted.

With one last glance at Amanda, he stepped forward, taking a coil of lights from Doc. The crowd quieted, watching as he dressed the tree, the lights casting a heavenly glow on his face.

Each movement he made was measured and deliberate, his respect for this tree and the town's new tradition apparent in how he handled each strand. These small moments, these little glimpses into who Jackson was, made Amanda's heart pound.

The tree lit up, bit by bit, until it stood glowing in the heart of the town's square, a beacon of holiday cheer. The sight was stunning, but Jackson, standing beneath the tree with a satisfied smile, took her breath away.

As the crowd erupted into applause, she knew she'd made the right choice. She had no idea what the future held but she wouldn't want to be anywhere else. Because here, with Jackson, everything felt right.

As tree lights twinkled and the town hung their ornaments, a collective sigh of awe swept through the crowd. The atmosphere was electric, the tree's luminescent glow adding a fairylike touch to the otherwise humble place. As if on cue, the first notes of a familiar melody floated through the air. One by one, people joined in, their voices blending into a heartwarming creation that filled the night with cheer.

The sound of the singing wrapped around Amanda like a hug. It was a picturesque moment to witness the people of Aspen Cove coming together to celebrate.

As the last strains of "Silent Night" echoed across the square, Maisey emerged from the diner with a tray filled with mugs of steaming hot cocoa. She moved through the crowd with practiced ease, passing out the warm drinks. Rich dark chocolate drifted through the air. It was a comforting and familiar scent that filled Amanda's heart with gratefulness.

While people warmed their hands and spirits on Maisey's cocoa, Katie appeared with a tray of homemade cookies. The sight of the baked goods brought forth smiles and eager hands, the sweet treats adding yet another layer to the celebration.

The caroling gave way to laughter and conversation, the square buzzing with energy as friends, family, and neighbors swapped stories and shared in the holiday spirit. Jackson was pulled into a conversation with a group of older men, but his laughter echoed over the sound of the bustling crowd.

She moved among them, a warm mug of cocoa in her hand, and wondered if Bea would be proud. She listened to tales of past holidays, laughed at old town legends, and shared her own stories. She realized she'd met and talked to everyone in town. They were now a part of her life and future.

Everybody here had their pasts, hopes and dreams, and heartaches. Yet tonight, under the glow of the holiday lights and in the comfort of shared goals, they were one.

It was in this small town, among these people, and with Jackson by her side, that she was beginning to feel like she was home. And as the last notes of a carol moved through the night, she knew, with a heart full of hope, that this was where she belonged.

The celebration in the town square wound down. Hand in hand, Amanda and Jackson made their way to the truck and back to the cabin.

Once inside, they shook off the winter chill, hanging their coats and kicking off their boots before sinking into the comfortable couch and relishing the feel of each other's company.

"Thank you," he said.

She laid her head on his shoulder. "Anything for love."

They spent the next hours reflecting on the day's events. They talked about the holiday songs they sang, the laughter, the sense of togetherness, and their feelings. The conversation flowed easily between them, as though they'd known each other for years instead of weeks.

As the evening deepened into night, they found themselves off the couch, out of their clothes, and naked in front of the fire. Amanda lay there as Jackson showed her how great a lover he was. He started with a kiss, exploring her curves with soft caresses, each touch eliciting a pleasured moan. His hands moved to her hips, waist, and shoulders until his fingers tangled in the curls of her hair.

Their bodies became entwined in a passionate and tender embrace, each movement expressing a deeper intimacy that could only be born from true love. As he entered her, Amanda was drawn closer to him with each stroke. She clung to him as the sensations of pleasure began to build.

The fire crackled in the background while their lovemaking played out in the foreground. With each thrust, the heat between them seemed to rise until they were both lost in an intense fog of bliss.

Time seemed to stand still as they moved together until, in one explosive finale, they reached the heights of ecstasy together. Gasping for breath, they slowly fell back into reality, their hearts pounding between sighs of contentment.

Jackson rolled off her and pulled Amanda close. Laying his head on her chest, he whispered, "I love you," as they lay there peacefully, basking in the afterglow of their lovemaking.

"I love you more," she said.

As night gave way to morning and the world slowly crept back in, Amanda knew that whatever life had in store for them, she was ready for it because here with Jackson was where she would stay.

CHAPTER TWENTY

Jackson stepped back and held the brush high in the air, admiring his work with a satisfied sigh. It had been a labor of love, transforming the worn and broken cabinets to their current renewed state.

He had spent days replacing panels, sanding, and then painstakingly applying multiple coats of low-VOC paint in a soft cream color. Amanda had been adamant that this would be the perfect shade to set off the rustic walls, and she was right. They were the perfect compliment.

Gunner stretched out next to the warm hearth while Catsby had found a comfortable spot on a chair, observing the proceedings with a curious eye.

Steam rose from the slow-cooked stew on the stove, a new recipe Amanda was trying. She was an excellent cook, and he loved their time together in the kitchen.

His gaze wandered to her, bathed in the soft light of her desk lamp, wholly engrossed in her writing. Her fingers paused over her keyboard as she turned to him. "Dinner will be ready soon."

He grinned at her, sniffing the air theatrically. "Smells amazing, sweetheart. Can't wait to try it."

Excitement filled her eyes. "I'm glad. And the paint ... it's okay for the animals to be here?"

Nodding his head, he chuckled. "It's low-VOC and safe for us and the pets. You can't even smell it."

She lifted her nose in the air. "You're right. All I smell is the stew." She returned to her screen, her fingers resuming their movement across the keyboard. He continued to watch her, intrigued by the intense focus she exhibited. He couldn't wait to read what she'd put hours of passion into writing, but it would remain a secret until Meg edited it and Amazon printed it.

After their meal, Jackson stood from the table and gathered the dishes. Amanda protested, but he shook his head with a smile. "You cooked. I clean. It's only fair."

As he cleaned the dishes, Amanda leaned against the counter, her arms crossed. "You did a great job with the cabinets, Jackson. They look amazing."

He glanced back at her, offering a smile. "Thank you. I'm glad you like them."

Just before he left for his shift, he pulled her close, pressing a lingering kiss to her lips. "I'll see you when I get back, sweetheart." She returned to her computer to type as he slipped out the front door.

AT THE BAR, the welcoming atmosphere warmed Jackson. He enjoyed the friendly banter with the regulars and the stories they shared. As the evening wore on, Doc entered the bar, his eyes alight with the promise of competition.

ONE HUNDRED MERRY MEMORIES

"Ready to lose another game, Jackson?" Doc taunted, sliding onto a stool.

Jackson laughed, shaking his head. "Not tonight, Doc. Tonight is my night."

As they began their tic-tac-toe game on the countertop, Doc started conversing about the town's Christmas tree. "That was a beautiful sight. The tree, all lit up."

Jackson nodded, his eyes on the makeshift game board. "It was a special moment."

Doc paused, giving him a knowing look. "You two seem quite taken with each other." Doc finished the game quickly, winning his nightly beer as usual. Jackson poured him a frosted mug.

Jackson's heart warmed at the thought of Amanda. "I can't deny that Doc. She's ... she's something else."

Doc nursed his beer as he looked at Jackson. "You seem happy, son. This life suits you."

Jackson paused, a soft smile gracing his lips as he thought of Amanda. "I am Doc. I never thought I could be this content."

Doc raised an eyebrow, a glint of curiosity in his eyes. "Ever think about making it more permanent? Marriage, children?"

Jackson laughed, remembering Doc's earlier advice. "Now, didn't you tell me to take things slow?"

Doc chuckled, taking a long sip of his beer. "Yep, you got me there. I love having you two here. Marriage and babies seem to keep people in place."

"We aren't going anywhere." He couldn't imagine himself in another town, living in another home, or being with another woman. Amanda, the cabin, and Aspen Cove were all he needed. And the babies, those would come when the time was right. He was certain.

As the night progressed, the bar started to thin out, each patron heading home. Doc was one of the first to leave, giving Jackson a friendly pat on the back before making his way home in time to watch *Dancing with the Stars* with Agatha, whom he called Lovey.

Soon enough, it was just him, Red, and Viv. Viv was a fiery woman with a quick wit, who, along with her boyfriend Red, had become family to Jackson. Viv was the first person he'd met when his truck broke down on the side of the road, and she felt terrible for his dog and gave them a ride into town.

She swirled her drink as she stared at him. "You know, it's funny how life works, right?"

Jackson looked at her, raising an eyebrow as he wiped down a nearby table. "How so?"

She gestured between herself and Red, then back to Jackson. "None of us came here looking for love. Red and I were just here for business, and you were here to start over. Yet, here we are, all warm, fuzzy, and smitten."

Jackson laughed, shaking his head. "Must be something in the air."

"Must be," Viv replied, her gaze softening. "But happy looks good on you, Jackson."

They finished their drinks and left him alone to lock up. Jackson made his way home, Viv's words echoing in his mind. He was happy and in love, and like he promised Doc, he was staying.

He entered the cabin to find Amanda fast asleep at her desk with her hand on the laptop keyboard. The words 'The End' were displayed on the screen. As he woke her and took her to bed, he hoped the characters she created would find the same joy and love he had found in her arms.

CHAPTER TWENTY-ONE

Amanda paced the living room of the secluded cabin, the cool hardwood under her bare feet a stark contrast to the heat radiating from the lit fireplace. It was a different kind of anticipation today, not like any of her previous book releases. This one was personal, more meaningful somehow. She couldn't keep still, her heart fluttering with every rustle of leaves or crack of a twig outside, half-expecting it to be the delivery truck she was anxiously awaiting.

Catsby meowed in protest of her sudden movements, weaving around her ankles as if attempting to calm or trip her and stop the endless pacing. Amanda stooped to scratch the cat behind his ears, the purring a soothing balm to her restless spirit.

Gunner chose to observe the spectacle from the comfort of his rug by the fireplace, too tired from the morning's walk to partake in the excitement. His brown eyes followed Amanda, his tail thumping against the floor at her occasional reassuring smiles.

Desperate to ease her nerves, she called Meg. Her

friend's voice was always a grounding force in her whirlwind of emotions.

"Hey, Meg," Amanda exhaled into the phone, pressing it against her ear as she continued her restless pacing.

"Has it arrived?"

"No," she said in exasperation before walking three more lengths of the room.

"I can hear you. Have you left a worn path on the floor yet?" The sound of Meg's laughter eased the tension. "You've done this before, remember?"

A small smile tugged at Amanda's lips. "I know, but this feels different. It's ... it's Aspen Cove."

"I get it. It's a piece of you. But remember, you've written a brilliant book, and I can't wait for the next one. Trust me. The world needs more of what you offer."

A sudden rustle outside had Amanda's heart leaping. "Meg, I think it's here! I'll call you back!" She hurriedly ended the call, leaving Catsby in her wake as she rushed toward the window, hoping to see the long-awaited delivery truck. However, she only found that pesky raccoon who habitually looked in the windows as if begging to return.

Seeing her anxiety, Jackson tried to bring her back into the present moment. "Why don't we focus on our special Christmas Eve plans? That'll help keep your mind off waiting."

Amanda turned toward him. "What plans?"

"Did you forget about the Christmas cookie hop we talked about?"

Recognition flashed in Amanda's eyes. "Oh my God, yes. I did." Every family in Aspen Cove was supposed to bake a batch of cookies and go to Main Street to sample them.

"I thought so, which is why I'm about to get started on our batch."

He gestured toward the kitchen, where a jumble of ingredients lay waiting on the counter. The oven was preheating, filling the cabin with a comforting warmth opposite to the chilly winter outside.

"Would you come and help me?" he asked, his eyes pinning her with a playful challenge. "I could use the company. Maybe the distraction would do you some good."

A small smile tugged at the corners of her lips, and her mind steered away from her book. She gave a decisive nod with a thoughtful glance at the waiting kitchen. "Alright, let's do this. Christmas in Aspen Cove wouldn't be complete without a proper cookie hop."

With the promise of the warm, shared activity, the cabin was filled with a new kind of vitality—the start of a new tradition and the joy of a group event. And the delivery of her book took a comfortable backseat to the delightful prospect of baking Christmas cookies with Jackson.

With newfound determination, Amanda tied an apron around her waist and joined him in the kitchen. They embarked on the cookie-making journey, a dash of laughter and a sprinkle of playful banter being ingredients just as crucial as the flour and sugar they worked with.

They fell into a rhythm, Amanda mixing the dry ingredients while Jackson whipped up the wet ones. He'd occasionally sneak a bit of cookie dough, grinning like a child when Amanda would swat his hand away, scolding him about salmonella risks. Their smiles were bright and genuine, the kitchen brimming with lightheartedness.

Catsby hopped onto a stool, watching them with intrigue, while Gunner wagged his tail happily, hoping for any dropped goodies.

The cookie dough was soon ready, and they painstakingly shaped it into little rounds, Jackson even attempting to make a few in the shape of Christmas trees, their forms more abstract than accurate. Amanda laughed at his attempt, her worries forgotten in the shared joy of the task.

Finally, the cookies were slid into the oven, the cabin filling with the richness of sweets. They waited, watching the cookies rise, their golden edges promising deliciousness and decadence.

Just as the oven timer rang, announcing the cookies' readiness, the screech of brakes outside shattered the serene atmosphere. Amanda's heart raced. She recognized that sound—the delivery truck.

She rushed to the door, flinging it open to see the delivery man lifting a large box. It was here—her novel. The sight made her breath catch. The moment she'd been waiting for had arrived. As Jackson pulled the cookies from the oven, the cabin filled with the scent of sweet success—baked cookies and her completed novel.

With shaky hands, she tore open the box, the cardboard giving way to reveal the culmination of her dedication and hard work. She pulled out a copy, its fresh pages smelling of new print and dreams. The cover was stunning, capturing the essence of Aspen Cove in vibrant colors.

Her fingers traced the title and her new pen name, Kelly Collins. She glanced up at Jackson, who was eyeing the book with curiosity.

"Why Kelly Collins?" he asked, leaning against the kitchen counter, a still-warm cookie in his hand.

She shrugged, a playful smile tugging at her lips. "Kelly, for the green color of the pines in Aspen Cove. And Collins, well ... it's got good alliteration, don't you think?"

Jackson chuckled, taking a bite of his cookie. "It does."

His gaze moved to the title. "*One Hundred Reasons* ... What's it about?" he asked.

Warmth spread in Amanda's chest as she considered her answer. She ran a hand over the glossy cover, her smile tender. "It's about real life, Jackson. Real people. It's about love, hope, and resilience. It's about the trials and tribulations that the world throws our way, and the strength we find to overcome them. It's about the power of a small town, of a tight-knit community. It's about Aspen Cove."

Jackson was quiet, a softness in his eyes as he looked at her. "I can't wait to read it," he said, his voice filled with sincerity.

Aspen Cove, their life here, was a story that needed to be shared with the world, and with Sage's and Cannon's blessing, she started where Bea's gifts began.

With the opened box now sitting on their kitchen table, Amanda turned to Jackson. "You up for some Christmas elf work?"

He arched a brow. "Depends. Do the elves get cookies?"

Laughing, she swatted at his arm. "I'll give you more than cookies."

"In that case, I'm in."

They spent the rest of the afternoon wrapping the books in festive paper, complete with red and green bows. It was a task that should have been tedious, but with Jackson by her side, cracking terrible jokes and singing off-key Christmas carols, it was anything but. Gunner and Catsby kept them company. One curled up by the fireplace and the other perched on a kitchen chair, watching everything with the curiosity only a cat can muster.

Once the books were neatly bundled, they lovingly

placed them into sturdy boxes, preparing for their journey to town. The air in Aspen Cove was infused with the spirit of Christmas. Laughter echoed through the air, intermingling with the jingle of bells and the merry tunes of carolers. The small-town ambiance embraced them, wrapping them in holiday cheer.

With each step, the tantalizing scent of freshly baked cookies wafted around them, as if the very essence of Christmas had been captured in these delightful treats. The town's residents, dressed in holiday sweaters and festive hats, shared their culinary creations with joy and excitement.

Friends and neighbors hopped from shop to shop, their hands holding plates brimming with an array of cookies, from buttery sugar cookies adorned with vibrant icing to fragrant gingerbread men with delicate icing smiles.

As she and Jackson handed out the gift-wrapped books, the reaction from the townsfolk was overwhelmingly positive. Smiles spread across faces, surprised gasps filled the air, and more than one person hugged Amanda, their eyes filled with happiness.

By the time they finished delivering the books and cookies, dusk had settled, and the twinkling Christmas lights illuminated the streets, painting a picture that Amanda knew she would cherish forever.

With their tasks for the day completed, they, along with Gunner in tow, made their way toward the cemetery. The last rays of the setting sun bathed the landscape in a golden hue, turning the snow-covered grounds into an expanse of peace and serenity.

Amanda walked up the hill to Bea's grave, her heart heavy but full. Kneeling, she placed a copy of her book by the headstone, her fingers brushing over the etched letters of Bea's name. "Hey, Bea," she whispered, the wind carrying her words.

Her throat tightened, emotions swirling within her. "Thank you. For everything," she started, her voice shaky. "You changed my life. You changed all our lives. Aspen Cove ... it wouldn't be what it is without you." She pointed to the book. "This is because of you. Because of this place you loved, and the people you cared for."

Beside her, Jackson placed a comforting hand on her shoulder, his silence a strong presence.

"I found the desire to write again. Most importantly, I found love," she added, "in more ways than I could've imagined. I found it in this town, its people, the quiet of the woods, and Jackson."

She took a deep breath, her words echoing in the expanse of the cemetery. She was silent as if letting her words settle, allowing the appreciation to seep into the ground beneath them, reaching Bea wherever she was.

As they headed back under the emerging stars, they were quiet. The stillness surrounding them seemed to encapsulate the serenity within their hearts. It was a journey of ups and downs and unexpected turns and surprises. But as they neared their cabin with the golden light from the windows guiding them, Amanda was filled with contentment.

"I love you, Jackson," she said, her voice soft but firm. "And I can't wait to see what the future holds for us."

Jackson squeezed her hand in response. "I love you too, Amanda. And whatever the future brings, we'll face it together."

The final words hung in the air as they stepped into

their home with the promise of more stories, more adventures, not yet written but eagerly anticipated. Aspen Cove had given them the freedom to love, live, and laugh, and they were ready for whatever came their way. They stepped into the next chapter of their lives with happiness in their hearts, hope in their eyes, and so much more to explore.

A NOTE FROM THE AUTHOR

Wow, you got through twenty-four books. Twenty-five if you count the prequel, *One Hundred Moments*. That's quite an accomplishment. And if you started at the end, I would implore you to go back to the beginning and see how we got here. As I considered the conclusion to the series, I thought it would be lovely if a writer such as myself brought the series full circle, and that's why Amanda entered the story. I still think it was a brilliant ending, and I hope you do too.

The bulk of my career has been spent writing books in Aspen Cove. I got the inspiration while visiting Estes Park, Colorado. It's a small town that's quite a tourist destination but a place I visit every summer. The thing about it is, I've never felt like a stranger there but a friend no one has met.

When I wrote *One Hundred Reasons*, it was entirely out of my norm. I'd been writing steamy romance for several years, so toning down the intimacy was a challenge at first. Still, I loved how I could replace all that with something equally emotional and profoundly beautiful—love in its rawest and purest form. The deep connections, the shared dreams, and the resilience of the human spirit. That's what Aspen Cove has come to embody, and I'm forever grateful that you've embarked on this journey with me.

Over the years, we've met incredible characters, faced heartbreaking moments, and shared joyous celebrations. Aspen Cove became more than just a setting for these stories. It became a home—our home. With every word, chapter, and book, we've woven an elaborate tapestry of lives, love, and second chances.

Your messages, comments, and love for the characters and their stories have driven every page I've written. Each character holds a piece of my heart and knowing that they've touched yours in some way makes every late-night writing session, every moment of writer's block, and every hurdle crossed worth it.

I want to express my deepest gratitude as we bid farewell to Aspen Cove. Thank you for your unwavering support and passion for these stories and for becoming a part of this journey. Without you, Aspen Cove would be a collection of words. You've brought these characters and their stories to life with enthusiasm, tears, and laughter.

While we're turning the last page of Aspen Cove, it's not goodbye. It's a celebration of the journey we've shared, the friendships we've formed, and the love we've found. As I move on to new adventures in my writing career, I hope you'll join me, carrying the spirit of Aspen Cove in our hearts.

So, here's to you, the reader, the dreamer, the believer. Here's to every sunrise we've welcomed and every sunset we've bid farewell in Aspen Cove. Here's to love, second chances, and the magic of small-town romance.

Thank you, from the bottom of my heart, for being a part of the Aspen Cove series. Until our next adventure together, happy reading!

Always choose love,

Kelly

BEA'S HOLIDAY FEAST

Bea's Beautiful Pineapple-Glazed Ham

No celebration in Aspen Cove is complete without Bea's pineapple-glazed ham. The leftovers would make great sandwiches ... if there were any leftovers.

1 7-9 lb fully-cooked, bone-in ham
1 ½ cup pineapple juice
1 cup brown sugar
1 tbsp Dijon mustard
¼ tsp ground cloves
1 can pineapple slices
I jar maraschino cherries without stems
Toothpicks

Preheat oven to 325 degrees.

Set the ham cut-side down in a large roasting dish. Make the ham pretty by attaching the pineapple slices (using the toothpicks) all over the ham, in whatever pattern you please.

Again, using the toothpicks, affix a cherry in the middle of each pineapple slice. This is your masterpiece, so have fun with it!

Bake the ham for 30 minutes. While baking, put the glaze ingredients into a small saucepan and bring to a boil. Reduce the heat and simmer for 10-15 minutes, until the mixture reduces to a syrup. Remove from burner.

After the initial 30 minutes of baking time, remove the ham from the oven. Brush glaze over the ham. Return to the oven and bake for another 30 minutes. Remove from oven, and brush additional glaze on the ham. Return to oven and bake for an additional 30 minutes. Remove again and brush the remaining glaze over the top of the ham. Return to oven and bake until a meat thermometer reads 140 degrees, about 30 more minutes.

Remove your masterpiece from the oven. Don't forget about all of those toothpicks when you start slicing!

Bacon Me Crazy Green Beans with Bacon
Bacon. Need I say more?

6 slices bacon, raw, chopped
1 1/2 pound green beans, trimmed
1/2 cup diced yellow onion
2 garlic cloves, minced
1 cup chicken broth
1/2 teaspoon salt
1/2 teaspoon black pepper

Cook the bacon in a large skillet or Dutch oven (with a

tightly-fitting lid, which you'll need later) until browned. Remove from pan and keep warm.

Add the onion and garlic to the pan and cook until the garlic starts to sing (about 2 minutes). Stir in the green beans. Add the chicken broth, give it a final stir, and cover the pan. Reduce heat to low, and cook for one hour, or until the green beans are tender. Stir in the bacon and cook just until you're sure you aren't serving your guests cold bacon in their beans.

Mouthwatering Mashed Potatoes

Can mashed potatoes make a person swoon? If you say no, you've never tried these potatoes.

4 lbs Russet or Yukon Gold potatoes, peeled and quartered
½ cup butter, melted
4 cloves, minced garlic
1 cup cream or half and half, warmed
Salt and pepper to taste

Place the potatoes and minced garlic in a large pot and add enough water to cover the potatoes. Bring the pot to a boil, then reduce heat slightly. Boil until the potatoes are tender. Turn off heat and drain potatoes. Add the butter and mash the potatoes with a potato masher. Slowly stir in the warm cream until incorporated. Salt and pepper to taste.

Sweet on You Sweet Potato Casserole

Not a fan of sweet potatoes? This dish is sure to change your mind. Everything is better with a streusel topping.

3 lbs sweet potatoes, peeled and cut into 1-inch cubes
1 cup cream or half and half

½ cup brown sugar
1 tsp salt
1 tsp vanilla
2 eggs, lightly beaten

Topping:
2 cups miniature marshmallows
½ cup flour
¼ cup brown sugar
¼ tsp salt
2 tbsp butter

Preheat oven to 375.

Boil the sweet potatoes until tender. Drain and allow the potatoes to cool slightly (no one wants scrambled eggs in their sweet potatoes). Mash the potatoes. Stir in cream, brown sugar, salt, vanilla and eggs until combined and smooth.

Spread in a greased 9X13 pan or large casserole dish. Top with mini marshmallows (feel free to pop a few in your mouth to make sure they're fresh). Mix the flour, brown sugar, and salt together in a small bowl. Cut in the butter and sprinkle the crumbly mixture on top of the mini marshmallows.
Bake for 30 minutes.

Sugar Cookies

These crisp sugar cookies are perfect to take to a gathering or share with friends ... if they make it out of the house...

1 cup powdered sugar
1 cup granulated sugar
1 cup butter
1 cup vegetable oil
2 eggs
1 tsp vanilla
1 tsp almond extract
4 cups flour
1 tsp salt
1 tsp baking soda
1 tsp cream of tartar
1 tsp almond extract

Using mixer, blend sugars, butter, oil and eggs. Add remaining ingredients. Chill dough for 30-60 minutes.

Preheat oven to 350 degrees. Roll dough into 1-inch balls and place on parchment paper lined baking sheet. Flatten with a glass dipped in sugar.

Bake for 8-10 minutes. Remove from oven. Allow to cool for a few minutes, then remove cookies and place on a baking rack to finish cooling.

Delicious Pumpkin Dump Cake

"Dump cake" is such an ugly name for this rich, amazing comfort dish. You will be the most popular person at every gathering if you bring this super-simple dessert (and you don't have to tell anyone how easy it was).

1 15 oz can pumpkin puree (NOT pumpkin pie mix!)
12 oz can evaporated milk

3 large eggs, lightly beaten
1 cup brown sugar
2 tsp pumpkin pie spice
1 box yellow cake mix
½ cup chopped pecans (optional)
1 cup butter, melted
Whipped cream (optional)

Preheat oven to 350. Grease a 9X13 baking dish.

In a large bowl combine the pumpkin, evaporated milk, eggs, brown sugar, and pumpkin pie spice. Spread into the prepared baking pan. Sprinkle the cake mix over the top of the pumpkin mixture. Sprinkle the pecans over the top if you're adding them. Drizzle the melted butter over top of everything.

Bake for 45-50 minutes, until the center is set and the edges are browned. Although it's amazing served warm, it is delicious at room temperature, too!

OTHER BOOKS BY KELLY COLLINS

Recipes for Love

A Taste of Temptation

A Pinch of Passion

A Dash of Desire

A Cup of Compassion

A Dollop of Delight

A Layer of Love

Recipe for Love Collection 1-3

Recipe for Love Collection 4-6

The Second Chance Series

Set Free

Set Aside

Set in Stone

Set Up

Set on You

The Second Chance Series Box Set

A Pure Decadence Series

Yours to Have

Yours to Conquer

Yours to Protect

A Pure Decadence Collection

Wilde Love Series

Betting On Him

Betting On Her

Betting On Us

A Wilde Love Collection

The Boys of Fury Series

Redeeming Ryker

Saving Silas

Delivering Decker

The Boys of Fury Boxset

Making the Grade Series

The Dean's List

Honor Roll

The Learning Curve

Making the Grade Box Set

Stand Alone Billionaire Novels

Dream Maker

Click here to see all of Kelly Collins' novels

GET A FREE BOOK.

Go to www.authorkellycollins.com

ABOUT THE AUTHOR

International bestselling author of more than thirty novels, Kelly Collins writes with the intention of keeping love alive. Always a romantic, she blends real-life events with her vivid imagination to create characters and stories that lovers of contemporary romance, new adult, and romantic suspense will return to again and again.

Kelly lives in Colorado at the base of the Rocky Mountains with her husband of twenty-seven years, their two dogs, and a bird that hates her. She has three amazing children, whom she loves to pieces.

For More Information
www.authorkellycollins.com
kelly@authorkellycollins.com

Printed in Great Britain
by Amazon